THE INCR~ Jake Parker

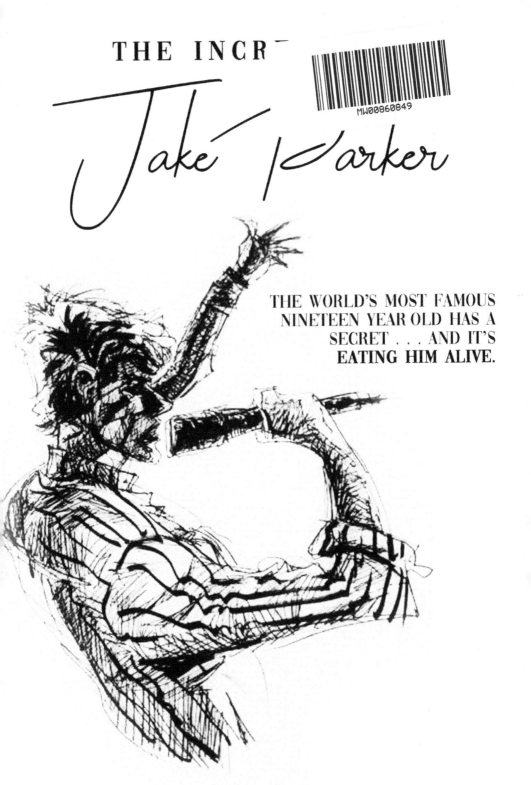

THE WORLD'S MOST FAMOUS
NINETEEN YEAR OLD HAS A
SECRET . . . AND IT'S
EATING HIM ALIVE.

ANGELO THOMAS

This book is dedicated to the millions of incredible people around the world who suffer in silence from anorexia, bulimia, and other forms of eating disorders. May you feel represented and understood by *The Incredible Jake Parker*, and may you find the strength and courage within yourself to speak up about your struggles and to take appropriate action in your own pursuit of a life worth living.

YOUR FUTURE IS WORTH FIGHTING FOR

"Angelo Thomas' insightful debut novel gets at the heart of how eating disorders can develop among young people, and it shows how eating disorders can be successfully addressed through treatment and community support. Whether someone is coming to grips with the possibility of an eating disorder, is actively working to recover from one, or knows someone affected by one, ANAD is grateful for a story like *The Incredible Jake Parker*, which offers an important and hopeful perspective on recovery from anorexia."

–Lynn Slawsky, Executive Director, ANAD (National Association of Anorexia Nervosa and Associated Disorders)

The National Association of Anorexia Nervosa and Associated Disorders (ANAD) is the oldest organization dedicated to fighting eating disorders in the United States and is a non-profit organization that works in the areas of support, awareness, advocacy, referral, education, and prevention.

To learn more about ANAD, including its free support services and opportunities for you to be involved in supporting its mission, visit www.ANAD.org.

The Center
for Balanced Living

"Jake Parker's story is a testament to the highs and lows that permeate life with an eating disorder. Whether denial that life has spun beyond one's control or that first glimmer of hope for a life worth living, Angelo's characters are true to form. The truth of the matter is that eating disorders affect people from every walk of life: persons of every race, ethnicity, age, sexual identity and orientation . . . and yes, even rock stars. The most important point of this book is that diagnosis of an eating disorder does not determine one's fate. Indeed, the spirit of a human being, strong, convicted and determined, can overcome anything – including an eating disorder.

"Angelo Thomas draws upon his own life in assuming an important role in illuminating the journey of warrior proportion to overcome an eating disorder. With the telling of his own story in his documentary, *To a Life Worth Living*, and now in telling Jake Parker's story, Angelo has arisen as an important spokesperson for people who struggle with eating disorders.

"As President and CEO of The Center for Balanced Living, there is nothing that warms the heart more than to see a patient who emerges in recovery as an advocate for people with these heavily misunderstood and deadly conditions.

"Having worked with healthcare activists around the world, I can say that Angelo possesses the heart of an advocate and the will to move positive change. My hope is that Angelo's work to raise awareness about life with an eating disorder and the related barriers will save the lives of many more for years to come."

–Kelly Trautner, President & CEO,
The Center for Balanced Living

The Center for Balanced Living is the only free-standing, non-profit organization in Ohio that provides specialized treatment for eating disorders.

The Center is dedicated to to specializing in evidence-based treatment, education and prevention, and research in eating disorders and to foster balance in the lives of all persons served.

To learn more about The Center for Balanced Living, visit www.centerforbalancedliving.org.

THE INCREDIBLE

Jake Parker

ONE

"Our next performer is a platinum-selling artist who took the world by storm with the release of his debut album late last year. Please welcome to the stage singer, songwriter, and pop music superstar Jake Parker."

That was sixth months ago at one of the biggest award shows in the music industry. Tyra Banks – yes, *that* Tyra Banks – introduced me to a crowd of thousands of people and at least a million more watching from home.

That was one of the coolest, most surreal moments of my nineteen years on this planet so far. I had my guitar in hand. I was singing my most popular song. It was everything I could have hoped for.

Now, I'm sitting in a restaurant in Los Angeles with Cat Carter, the person I spend more time with now than anyone else. She's not family, but she's the closest thing I have to that since I moved out here. She's actually my manager. I tell her everything. Well, almost everything. There's one thing I haven't told her or anyone else about yet. I've done everything I can to keep it a secret, but I have a feeling Cat knows. Kind of like how a parent knows their kid is gay but waits to say anything about it until they're ready to come out.

Cat already knows my secret. I can tell by the way she looks at me, even by the way she's looking at me right now. Like I'm a dead, depressing reminder of the person I was sixth months ago.

1

"You need to eat," Cat tells me as she dips a greasy curly fry in ketchup and tosses it into her mouth.

I look down at the plate in front of me and shake my head no. I already ate one bite out of my burger (without the bun) and three curly fries. No, wait. Four curly fries. Shit, I lost track. I'll log it as five just to be safe.

"I'm not hungry," I say, which isn't even a lie.

I don't remember the last time I really felt hungry. It's like that part of your brain that's supposed to tell you when you're hungry got tired of me ignoring it, so it just gave up on me.

"Jake," Cat says in an even more assertive tone than usual, "I can't do this anymore."

What the hell does that mean? What can't she do anymore? Why is she being so dramatic?

"I can't keep covering for you and pretending like everything's fine," she says. "People are starting to notice, Jake."

I try to say something to smooth things over, but Cat doesn't let me speak.

"You need help," she says, on the verge of tears now. "This isn't about your music or your career anymore, it's about your *life*."

"I'm fine," I insist, although she knows that isn't true. "You're blowing this way out of proportion."

"I don't think you understand how serious this is," she fires back. "Do you know which mental illness has the highest mortality rate? Anorexia."

Anorexia. I can't believe she said it. I can't believe someone actually said it out loud to me. That word has been on the tip of my tongue for months. It like, literally haunts me. I still can't admit to having an eating disorder, even after she just called me out on it.

"I'm not anorexic."

"Then eat."

I look down at my plate again.

Six months ago, I could've done this. I would've enjoyed it, too. This used to be my favorite restaurant in L.A. I would insist on bringing my sister Jule here every time she visited me, even if we weren't hungry. That's how much I liked it.

Now, I can't bring myself to take another bite of out of my burger or even eat another curly fry. Oh, and there's no way I'm eating the bun. Too many carbs.

Cat abruptly gets up from her seat at the table.

"I'm not doing this anymore," she says, her eyes welling up with tears. "You're getting help, Jake."

She grabs her purse and walks out of the restaurant, leaving me alone at the table. I hear the sound of Cat's heels briskly walking away until she's gone, and it's like everything else just disappears.

TWO

The next thing I know, I'm at a doctor's office. I hate doctors. Cat made me come. I couldn't change her mind.

I'm standing in front of a scale. In place of my trademark black skinny jeans and button-up shirt is a hospital gown. What a look.

"Go ahead and step on the scale for me please," the nurse standing behind me says.

It's amazing how many different thoughts go through my mind in that one moment. What happens if I'm underweight? What happens if I'm not? Or even worse, what if I'm actually *over*-weight? I don't know, and I don't want to know. I close my eyes, hoping that when I open them, I'll be somewhere else and this will all just go away.

When I open my eyes, I realize that I can't see the number on the scale. The nurse has it covered up with a sheet of paper. She doesn't tell me the number, but she makes a face as she makes note of it on the paperwork on her clipboard.

Once we're in the exam room, the nurse tells me that she has some questions for me about my "condition" before the doctor will see me.

"My condition?" I ask defensively, as if I have no clue why I'm here or what's been going on with me for the past six months. "There's nothing wrong with me."

The nurse just gives me a threatening look that tells me she knows that isn't true. She begins to ask me questions from a sheet attached to her clipboard.

"Are you depressed?"

"Maybe? I don't know."

"Are you happy with your current weight?"

"Is anyone?"

"How much weight do you think you've lost in the past six months?"

"I don't know."

"Do you believe you have an eating disorder?"

That's the one question I don't answer. I'm beyond irritated now. I shouldn't have to be here. I stare at the floor, avoiding eye contact with the nurse. I hate her.

She makes some marks on her clipboard and sighs.

"Dr. Holden will be in in a few minutes," the nurse says as she leaves the room. "Make yourself comfortable."

Someone I met five minutes ago, who knows nothing about me, has been grilling me about something I've never talked about, and I'm sitting on a cold examination table in a doctor's office wearing a hospital gown that looks like a pillowcase. *Make myself comfortable.* Right.

I stare at the clock on the wall, and all I notice for the next few minutes is the sound of it ticking. It irritates me, but I don't why, which just irritates me even more.

Suddenly there's a knock at the door, and in walks the main attraction of this shitshow, Dr. Holden.

"Hi Jake, I'm Dr. Holden," he says, as if that weren't obvious already.

He shakes my hand. Have you ever shaken someone's hand and felt like you could immediately tell how you felt about them? Yeah, me too. I hate this guy.

"I wanted to start by sharing something with you," he says as opens the laptop he carried in and pulls something up on the screen.

He turns the screen around for me to see, and I'm looking at a graph of my height and weight since I was like, twelve. I don't remember signing a release form for that information to some random doctor, but maybe I'll bring that up later.

"This is how much weight you've dropped since you turned eighteen," Dr. Holden says, "which is around the last time you saw your primary care doctor back home."

I stare straight at the graph on the laptop screen. There's a sharp decline at the end that represents how much weight I've lost. It's a lot. There's no way around that.

"I'm concerned about your health, Jake," Dr. Holden says. "You can't keep losing weight at this rate."

"Fine, I won't," I pretend to surrender. "I won't lose any more weight."

"You're severely underweight for your age, height, and gender," he reminds me. "I don't think maintaining is even an option for you at this point."

"I'm nineteen," I say, a bit more aggressive than I mean to. "It's my choice."

Isn't it, though? Why the hell should he or anyone else tell me how much I should weigh?

"It's your choice to be sick?" Dr. Holden asks. "It's your choice to be at risk for heart failure, osteoporosis, and even dying?"

"I'm not gonna die," I tell him. "I'm fine."

"I'd like to reach out to your parents to let them know what's going on."

I'm sorry, he wants to do *what* now? Talk to my parents? That's crossing a line.

"Absolutely fucking not!" I blurt out. "You can't do that. They don't need to know anything about this."

"They care about you, Jake," Dr. Holden says, talking to me like he's the host of *Intervention* on A&E and like I'm a fucking drug addict. "You have a whole village of people who care about you and who want to see you get better. The sooner you embrace that, the better your chance is of overcoming this."

Okay, sure, my parents care about me. They don't seem to care as much as they did when I was younger and they were still married, but like, that's normal, right?

7

Wait. Normal? Who am I kidding? My parents are anything but normal. My dad used to be the one with substance abuse issues, but now he's clean and my mom is the one with a drinking problem. They both care about something a lot more than they care about me. For my dad, that something is work, and for my mom, it's drinking. They like to change it up every few years though to keep me and my sister on our toes. God knows what they'll say when they find out about all of this.

"I'm going to refer you to a clinic in Phoenix, Arizona that specializes in treating eating disorders," Dr. Holden tells me. "I'm recommending you for residential treatment there."

"Residential?" I ask in disbelief. "For how long?"

"For as long as necessary," he says flatly.

"No way!" I fight back. "This isn't fair. You can't expect me to just stop my life."

"Your health has to become your priority," Dr. Holden insists. "Before your music, before your career. Before anything else."

THREE

I wish I weren't in the car with Cat right now, but I'm glad someone else is driving because L.A. traffic is literally is the worst. Cat clearly isn't in the mood for music or normal conversation. When Cat's quiet, nine times out of ten it's because she's pissed off about something.

"I swear to God, Cat," I finally say to break the silence, "I don't need this."

Cat ignores me, looking straight ahead with razor sharp focus even though we're stopped at a red light behind like, ten other cars.

"Just let it go," I say, sounding more desperate than I mean to. "Please."

Cat looks at me and takes off her sunglasses, probably to get a more accurate reading of me.

"I can't," she says. "I've been doing this for too long. I've seen it happen to too many people to let it happen to you, too."

What is *it* exactly? How many people could she possibly know with eating disorders? She's a talent manager for a record label for God's sake, not a psychologist.

"You can face this head on and get help," she tells me, "or you can keep lying to yourself about what's going on and lose everything you care about."

I can't believe she just said that.

"So you're threatening me now?" I ask, almost laughing at how ridiculous this conversation is getting.

"I'm telling you what your options are," Cat says. "Don't take what you have for granted."

She puts her sunglasses back on and looks ahead as we start moving again.

"That includes me," she says, stone cold but with some emotion buried underneath.

I come out of my room the next morning, and I can't believe who I see standing in the middle of my living room. It's my parents. Both of them. What. The. Fuck.

"I don't know how you can be surprised by any of this," my dad tells my mom.

"What the hell is that supposed to mean?" my mom asks defensively, crossing her arms.

"These things don't just come from nowhere, Sarah," my dad says. "There's a reason why Jake is the way he is."

"So what, I'm the reason?" My mom says, raising her voice. "You're saying it's my fault our son is sick?"

"Just look at him," my dad says, tossing his hand up towards me.

My mom turns around to face me, and I can see in her face that shock and sadness just hit her like a two-car train. She looks at me like I'm dead. My dad can't even look at me.

"Oh my god…" my mom says as I walk towards her. "Jake…"

"What are you doing here?" I ask because I don't know what else to say.

She doesn't answer my question though. She just hugs me, more tightly than she ever has, and she starts crying.

I make eye contact with my dad for just a second as I stand there, still hugging my mom. He looks away. I know why he can't look at me, but I don't care. I don't feel anything right now. Anger. Sadness. Nothing. I feel nothing.

"It's gonna be okay," my mom assures me, as if she has the power to just speak that into existence. "You're gonna be okay. We're here for you."

"You know, I should have known this would be too much," my dad says, shaking his head. "The music and the money and the fame. I should've stopped you. It's too much for a kid your age. And without us here to…"

His words trail off as he stops himself from getting emotional.

"Dad, this isn't your fault," I say. "It's nobody's fault."

11

Is it someone's fault though, I wonder? Is it all my fault? I don't know. It doesn't matter. I just don't want my parents to feel like this is their problem to solve because it's not. It's mine.

There's a knock on the door, and Cat walks in, carrying a binder and a box of tissues with her. Wait. I was joking when I made an *Intervention* reference earlier. God, please don't let this be an intervention. We don't need to give my parents an opportunity to be any more dramatic than they already are.

Cat offers the box of tissues to my mom, and she takes a couple. I wish my mom weren't crying right now.

"I just got off the phone with Dr. Holden," Cat tells me. "You've been approved for treatment in Phoenix."

"I'm sorry, who are you?" my dad asks, although I'm positive they've met at least once before.

"Dad, this is Cat," I say. "She's my manager."

Cat smiles and tries to shake my dad's hand but he doesn't flinch.

"Right," he says coldly. "Thanks for everything you've done for our son, but we'll take it from here."

"Excuse me?" Cat asks, stunned.

"This," my dad says, gesturing to the guitars and vinyl records displayed on the wall behind him, "never should have happened. I didn't stop it before, but I am now."

"You can't handle it," he says, looking directly at me.

"Yes I can," I say through gritted teeth.

"Then why did I have to come out here to see you?" my dad snaps back. "Why are we talking about you going to Phoenix?"

"Because…" I start to say, but I stop because I don't know what to say.

"Because you can't handle it," my dad says. "It's over, Jake. Your health has to come first."

I can't believe this is happening. I haven't seen my parents in almost a year, and now they're in my house telling me what to do like I'm a kid again? I need to get out of here before I break something or say something I'll regret. I shove my way past my dad and storm out of the room.

FOUR

I'm in my bedroom, still thinking about everything my parents said and everything I wish I'd said, when Cat comes in to check on me.

"You okay?" Cat asks, sitting next to me on the bed.

I nod. Yeah, I'm okay. Whatever. I just want to wake the fuck up from this god-awful nightmare.

"Look, I know this is a lot to take in," Cat says.

"My parents suck," I say.

"I won't argue with that," Cat sighs. "But you know what? This isn't about them. They'll only be around for a couple days, and then they'll go back to Seattle once you're in Phoenix. This is about you getting better. Do it for yourself and no one else. Okay?"

I feel like I'm weak if I just give in to everything she's saying, but deep down I know that she's right. I trust her.

"Okay," I say, and Cat hugs me from the side.

Cat opens the binder she brought in with her and gets out some paperwork for me to sign. She grabs a pen from the Seattle mug on my nightstand and hands it to me as I start skimming through the paperwork from the place in Phoenix.

"Everyone at the clinic signs an NDA," Cat assures me, "so don't worry about the press. No one outside of us has to know where you're going."

I can't imagine what would happen if everyone knew that I was going to residential treatment for an eating disorder. A guy with an eating disorder? And not just a guy, but Jake Parker of all people? What a fucking joke.

"When you're ready to come back, everything will still be here for you," Cat says. "I'll be here, and so will your fans. They may not know exactly what's going on, but they'll be rooting for you, Jake. We all will."

It sure as hell doesn't feel like everyone's rooting for me when I flip through channels on TV the next day. I was supposed to be going on tour in a couple of weeks, so of course anyone and everyone with a daytime talk show is talking about why I'm not going on tour now.

"Teenage girls everywhere are heartbroken as it was announced early this morning that singer-songwriter and teenage heartthrob Jake Parker will not go through with his previously announced world tour because of a 'serious health concern,'" Robin Roberts says on *Good Morning America*. "Neither Parker nor a representative from his label could be reached for comment, but our thoughts are with Parker and his family during this difficult time."

"Parker has mostly shied away from the spotlight over the past few months, but fans of his on social media have pointed out dramatic and concerning changes in Parker's appearance," Katie Couric says as a recent photo of me is shown on *The Today Show*.

"Is Jake Parker the latest celebrity to crack under the pressure of the entertainment industry?" Anderson Cooper asks on whatever show is on CNN.

"This could be the beginning of the end of his career," Whoopi Goldberg says to her co-hosts on *The View*. "We've seen it time and time again. It's horrible, but that's the cycle of this industry."

Finally, Meredith Viera asks the boldest fucking question she can think of in her segment on NBC News, "The question now is, is it even possible for Jake Parker to recover from this and rise back to the top?"

I don't know, Meredith. I guess we'll see, won't we?

FIVE

We're headed to Phoenix now, on our way to wherever the hell I'm going for treatment. I have time to look the place up online, but I don't. I don't want to accept that this is happening, even as we're literally getting closer and closer to that reality. This doesn't feel real.

I sit in the passenger's seat of the rental car my dad is driving, and I stare off into space, thinking about nothing and everything at the same time. My mom is in the back with Cat. Their interactions have been . . . interesting, to say the least.

"Can you shut that off please?" my mom hisses at one point as Cat texts away on her cell phone with keyboard clicks at full volume.

Cat totally overreacts, but she does silence her phone, which keeps my mom quiet for the rest of the ride because there's nothing else for her to complain about.

After what feels like the longest six-hour drive of my entire life, we finally arrive at the clinic called Path to Renewal. Ugh. You know how earlier I said that I can tell how I feel about someone right away? I guess I'm like that with places, too, because I already hate this place and I haven't even been inside yet. Just the sight of it makes me want to vomit. (I'm not bulimic though. That's a different eating disorder.)

My dad puts the car in park right in front of the hellish place. I notice he takes a deep breath before he unbuckles his seatbelt and gets out of the car, and then I get out, too.

My dad and I start to get my things out of the trunk. I just have a backpack and duffel bag because for some stupid reason, this place actually mandates how many bags you can bring with you. Whatever.

"You got it?" my dad asks, handing the duffel bag off to me, and I passively nod yes.

He comes closer to me, and I can tell he's getting ready to act like we have a good relationship and like he isn't thinking about the days he had to take off from work to be here.

"I don't say this enough, but I'm proud of you, son," my dad says. "I love you, and you're gonna get through this."

I don't think he could've phoned it in any more than that if he tried. That's literally the most generic thing he could have said to me.

He follows up that half-assed goodbye (or was it supposed to be more like a "good luck?") with a half-assed hug. That's my dad.

My mom's up next, and I already know she's about to one-up my dad by going way over-the-top with her goodbye. She probably spent the whole car ride here mentally preparing her speech.

"You are amazing and so, so brave," she says. "I know I haven't been the greatest mom . . . but I love you and I'm here for you, and I'm only ever just a phone call away."

Okay, that was actually not as dramatic as I was expecting. Look at you, Sarah, being in control of your emotions and shit.

"I love you," she says again, and she gives me a hug and a kiss on the cheek.

Next up is Cat, and I honestly don't know what to expect from her. I feel like this sort of thing is so out of her element, although I've seen more emotion from her these past few days than I ever did before.

"I know this isn't easy," Cat tells me, "and I know this may not be what you *want* to do right now, but I promise you'll be so much stronger because of it. You have your whole life ahead of you, Jake."

She starts tearing up again and hugs me. I actually kind of feel like crying, too, but I don't.

"You can do this," she says. "You can do anything. You've proven that."

That's the last thing anyone says to me before I walk into Path. I know this probably sounds dramatic, but I have no idea what's going to be happen from here on out. I don't know how long I'll be here, and I can't even say for sure that my life will be anything like it was before whenever I do get out of here.

19

I don't want to do this.

But fuck it, I'm doing it.

Here we go.

SIX

When I walk into Path, the first thing I see is a lobby that looks like a cross between a hotel lobby and the waiting area at a doctor's office. I walk up to the front desk.

"Good morning! What can I do for you?" the woman at the desk says to me with a smile.

"I'm, uh, starting treatment today," I say with none of the confidence that a platinum-selling pop star is supposed to have. "Residential."

She asks for my name, and I tell her. She doesn't seem to recognize me, and if she does, she doesn't say anything about it. Thank god. She attaches a questionnaire sheet to a clipboard and hands it to me over the desk.

"Go ahead and fill this out and take a seat over there," the woman says, gesturing towards dozens of empty chairs in the waiting area. "Your case manager will come to you shortly."

"Thanks," I say, although I'm not sure why I'm thanking someone for handing me a clipboard and telling me to sit down.

I take a seat and glance at the magazines sitting on the table next to me. They're all related to mental health. Who knew there were so many of these?

I look at the sheet on the clipboard I'm holding. I can tell I'm in for a ride here even before reading through all the questions. This is like the most on-the-nose eating disorder screening you could imagine.

I CONSTANTLY WORRY ABOUT MY WEIGHT AND/OR BODY SHAPE. (TRUE) (FALSE)

I circle True. I'm here, so I might as well answer honestly, right? I don't even know if anyone will look at this. Maybe it's just something to keep me busy while I wait for whoever my case manager is to show up.

I AM VERY AFRAID OF GAINING WEIGHT. (TRUE) (FALSE)

I feel like the first version of this just said "I am afraid of gaining weight," but someone thought to add the word "very" because it didn't sound eating disordered enough before. Whatever. I circle True.

I AM VERY DISSATISFIED WITH MY PHYSICAL APPEARANCE. (TRUE) (FALSE)

There's that word "very" again. Six months ago, I would have circled False. I can't pinpoint the specific moment that that changed, but I genuinely hate what I look like and I have for a while now. *Teenage heartthrob?* Yeah, that's not what I see. I circle True.

I MAKE MYSELF THROW UP (PURGE) AS A MEANS TO CONTROL MY WEIGHT AND/OR BODY SHAPE. (TRUE) (FALSE)

Nope. Nope. Nope. That's gross. False.

I USE DIURETICS AND/OR LAXATIVES AS A MEANS TO CONTROL MY WEIGHT AND/OR BODY SHAPE. (TRUE) (FALSE)

I've thought about it. Never tried it though. I'm not a pill person. I'm too good at losing weight to resort to shit like that anyway. I do (or did) it the old-fashioned way – by not eating as much. I circle False.

I FAST AS A MEANS TO CONTROL MY WEIGHT AND/OR BODY SHAPE. (TRUE) (FALSE)

Hey, speaking of not eating, here's one that actually applies to me. I mean, I eat. Obviously. Just like, not a lot. I track everything I eat on an app on my phone. Literally everything I ever eat. I don't drink anything with calories, but if I did, I would track those, too. Every calorie counts. I circle True.

I look up from the stupid questionnaire sheet as someone sits in the chair across from mine. She looks around my age. She's pretty, but I can tell that she's like me. I bet she goes out of her way to find clothes that can sort of hide how underweight she is. I can tell. I feel like when you have an eating disorder, you develop something like a gaydar, but like, a radar for people with eating disorders instead of for gay people. I like to think mine is pretty good.

Everything this girl is wearing looks like it came from Hot Topic. Even her jet-black hair and that dark, winged eyeliner. Fuck, she's so pale. And thin. I wish I were as thin as she is.

She's filling out a questionnaire on a clipboard just like the one I have. I wonder if she's starting today, too. I wonder if she knows I'm looking at her. She won't look at me. I can see in her face that this is the last place she wants to be right now. Me fucking too.

Mr. Case Manager finally decides to show up now, and the first thing I notice is how fucking saturated the green on his tie is. I'm not into it, man. Sorry.

If I had to put an age on him, he's probably in his early 40's. He's tall and kind of handsome in a TV sitcom dad kind of way. So like, not Zac Efron level handsome.

"Hi, you must be Jake," he says to me, shaking my hand like we're business partners or something.

I just nod. I wonder if he knows who I am. Maybe not. I guess a forty-year-old man with a dad bod isn't exactly in the target demographic for my music anyway.

"I'm Tim Benning," he says, finally letting go of my hand. "I'll be your therapist and case manager while you're here."

"Cool," I say for some reason.

I notice Hot Topic Girl look at me for the first time, her brow furrowed. I know what she's thinking. "Cool" is such a random-ass thing to say to meeting my case manager. Whatever.

"Cool," Tim echoes. "Okay, well if you don't mind following me upstairs, I can show you to your room and let you drop your things off before everyone heads to breakfast."

I feel my eye twitch a little at the mention of breakfast. I don't eat breakfast. I hate breakfast. This is great. Just fucking great.

"Okay, yeah," I force a smile, which I've gotten pretty good at doing since this all started. "Sounds good."

I don't think Tim buys the smile, but I don't care. I get up and follow Tim down the hall towards the stairs. I make eye contact with Hot Topic Girl again for a second before she looks away again.

I follow Tim Benning up the stairs and down the hall of the residence floor, and I glance into the rooms as we pass by them. They're pretty small, kind of like college dorm rooms. I don't see anyone in the rooms, but I feel like I get a decent sense of who they are based on what I see of their rooms. If I had to guess by the décor, they're mostly teenage girls, which is what I expected. I see some Lady Gaga and One Direction posters in one of the rooms, but none with Jake Parker. I don't know if I should feel relieved or disappointed about that.

"Am I the only guy?" I ask. "Like, are there any guys here besides me?"

"Well, there's me," Tim says with a stupid smile, "but no. We have five other clients in our residential program right now, and they're all girls and women."

"Gotcha," I say as we turn into a room near the end of the hall – my room.

There's a bunk bed and a table in there and not much else. It's as small as all the other rooms, but it feels really empty. Probably because it *is* empty. (Insert the guy face-palming emoji here.)

"But the good news is you get a room all to yourself," Tim says in a way that may or may not be sarcastic.

"*Great*," I say in a way that is definitely sarcastic.

"Yeah, so you can just set your things down here for now," Tim says. "We'll keep you engaged in activities throughout the day, so you won't spend much time in here."

I assume by "activities" that he means making me eat and lecturing me about eating to make me get fat. It's basically a reverse fat camp but with therapy and other psychological bullshit sprinkled on top.

"Cool," I find myself saying again for some reason.

EIGHT

I stand in front of the counter in the shared kitchen area on the first floor of Path. I'm staring at a microwaveable breakfast bowl, still frozen, from a brown paper bag with my name written on it.

Everyone else moves through the kitchen, each person making their own food in a separate microwave. I notice that only two of the four others fit the eating disordered stereotype of super thin, pale, and depressed teenage girls. Didn't Tim say there would be five other people besides me? Where's #5?

There are two professional watchdogs – "clinicians," they're called – in the room with us. They're both women, and I assume they're dietitians based on how closely they're watching us prepare our food. One of them walks over to me to introduce herself. She's probably in her late twenties and looks more approachable than the other one, but I think she could totally pass as a teenager if she were in a Disney Channel movie or on a show like *Glee*.

"Hi, I'm Jessica," she says, bubbling with an unexpected level of enthusiasm. "I'm your dietitian!"

"Hi," I say, a little turned off by how nice she is.

I don't hate her. I feel like if I met her six months ago, I would have wanted to be her best friend. I don't seem to vibe as well with people like her now though.

"So, for breakfast I have you down for a breakfast bowl, a banana, and eight ounces of whole milk," Jessica says. "If there's anything missing in your bag, let me know and I'll make you sure get everything."

It's kind of funny how she acts like she trusts me to tell her if I'm missing something that I'm supposed to eat. I mean, she's a dietitian working with people who have eating disorders. I can't imagine there's a very trusting client-clinician relationship there.

"Use one of the microwaves and follow the instructions on the label for your breakfast bowl," she tells me. "Sound good?"

I nod, and Jessica walks away to check on one of the other clients.

I glance down at the label on the breakfast bowl. The calorie number is marked out. Shit. I try not to let it faze me. I can probably look it up online later. I'm kind of glad I can't look it up now because I know I wouldn't eat it if I knew how many calories were in this thing.

I sit at the long, cafeteria-like table with the other clients, who are engaged in conversation and all seem to know each other pretty well. Jessica and the other dietitian are sitting with us, and they're eating, too, which actually makes me feel a little less uncomfortable for some reason.

I take a tiny sip from my glass of precisely eight ounces of whole milk. I can't believe how bad it tastes. How the hell does anyone drink this? I have to stop myself from gagging. I don't want to draw more attention to myself than I may already have just because of who I am.

I watch Jessica, who's sitting more towards to the other end of the table, as she mindlessly spreads cream cheese onto a bagel while chatting with the other clients. I can't help but cringe as she spreads more than twice the amount of cream cheese necessary onto one single bagel. Jesus Christ.

"That's so much cream cheese," someone to my left says. "I'm guessing at least fifty calories worth."

"No way," I say, my eyes still fixed on the bagel. "That's two tablespoons. A hundred calories minimum."

I turn to look at the calorie whisperer sitting next to me and realize that it's none other than Hot Topic Girl. I feel like an idiot for not noticing her before now. I didn't even see her come in, much less sit down right next to me.

"We don't count calories here," the other dietitian says to us. "That can be triggering for clients."

I glance at the ID card attached to the lanyard around her neck. Her name is Samantha Granger. "Registered Dietitian" is on the line under her name, but I feel like it would be more accurate if it said "Registered Bitch" instead. Ugh.

"Got it," Hot Topic Girl says, rolling her eyes.

I don't know much about Hot Topic Girl – hell, I don't even know her name – but I like her. I immediately register her as a badass.

"Is today your first day?" Hot Topic Girl asks me.

"Yup," I say, trying not to look as stoked to be talking to her as I am.

"Sweet, mine too," she says. "I'm Jordan."

"I'm Jake," I say.

Lauren, one of the girls sitting across from us, gasps. Has she been staring at me this whole time?

"Oh my god," she says.

"What?" Jordan asks, totally unamused.

"You're Jake Parker!" Lauren says. "Like, *the* Jake Parker. Oh my god, I knew it."

Fuck. I guess it was only a matter of time.

"That's me," I say, souding defeated like a *Scooby-Doo* villain who's just been unmasked in front of everyone.

"Dude, my little sister, she like adores you," Lauren says. "She's gonna *freak* when I tell her – "

Samantha clears her throat and gives Lauren a look that says "you better not."

"I mean . . . *Of course* I won't tell my sister that I'm in treatment with one of her favorite people in the world."

"Thanks," I say, feeling a little embarrassed.

I'm obviously used to people recognizing me and being the center of attention, but this is nothing like a group of teenage girls asking me to take a selfie with them in line at Starbucks. I don't want to be here period, and I especially don't want to be here as Jake Parker, the "singer, songwriter, and pop music superstar." I don't even feel like that's me anymore. Whatever.

One of the other clients, Lily, looks at me with a big, teethy smile. I know "teethy" is probably not a normal way to describe someone's smile, but if you saw it, trust me, you would understand. It's the kind of smile that's so obnoxious that it makes you never want to smile again. We're in an eating disorder clinic – what the hell is there to be smiling about like that?

"We're really glad you're here, Jake," Lily says to me with an uncomfortable amount of eye contact. "Don't worry, we can totally keep your secret."

Um. Okay. Thanks? Why do I feel like she's going to do the exact opposite though?

I exchange looks with Jordan, and I feel like she's thinking the same thing – I should try to keep my distance from Lily. Cat always says that first impressions are everything, and my first impression of Lily boils down to two words. Cryptic. Bitch.

NINE

We're all in the Group Room now, where I guess we'll do group therapy and shit like that. There's a seat for each of us and a few more, so I'm able to sit far enough from Cryptic Bitch Lily to feel comfortable. Well, as comfortable as I can be in a room decorated with posters with lame motivational quotes on them. There's a table in the middle of the room with paper, markers, and other arts & crafts supplies – you know, the essential supplies for forcing someone to recover from an eating disorder.

Carolyn, one of the other clinicians, comes in, and she's almost as annoying as Lily, the girl I'm actively avoiding. She's smiley and energetic like that mom who tries way too hard to be nice whenever you stay the night at your friend's house. That was never my mom. My mom's the kind of mom you don't let your friends meet because you don't want them to tell their parents how much alcohol she has just laying around the house.

I think about my mom too much. I wish I didn't. I wish I cared about her as little as she cares about herself. She's been a fucking trainwreck ever since she and my dad got divorced. I love her, but she was a lot to handle when I lived at home. I wish I could just move Jule out here and have her live with me because I just know that my mom is driving her crazy with her alcoholic, emotionally manipulative bullshit.

"Good morning, everyone!" Carolyn says, taking a seat between Lily and one of the other clients.

Carolyn immediately notices Jordan texting on her cell phone.

"Jordan," Carolyn says like a kindergarten teacher about to tell a kid to stop eating glue.

Jordan looks up at her, and she makes zero effort to hide how annoyed she is.

"It is Jordan, isn't it?" Carolyn asks.

Jordan nods.

"Could you turn your phone off and take it to your room during the next break?" Carolyn asks with an unnatural smile and too many blinks. "We don't use our phones during the day here."

"Suuuure," Jordan says, rolling her eyes and putting her phone away in the pouch of her hoodie.

"Before we get started with anything else," Carolyn says to the group, "I thought we could go around the room and have everyone introduce themselves by saying your name and a fun fact about yourself if you have one."

God, these people love to waste time on elementary school bullshit. There are so many other things I could be doing right now.

"I'll go first!" Lily says so cheerfully that I have to fight against the urge to vomit right then and there. (Okay, so I know this is the second time I've had to say it, but I swear I've never made myself throw up on purpose.)

"Go for it," Carolyn says, bouncing off of Lily's bizarrely consistent enthusiasm.

"Hi, my name is Lily, and a fun fact about me is that I'm going to school to be a nurse because I love helping people!"

"How are you in school if you're here?" Jordan asks, but she seems more annoyed than genuinely interested in this girl's life.

"I had to take a semester off," Lily explains, "but don't worry, I'll be back in school in the fall!"

"I wasn't worried," Jordan says flatly.

Lily looks caught off guard by that, but she quickly recharges and reverts back to her annoying, happy self just a moment later.

"Why don't you two go next?" Carolyn says to me and Jordan.

I look at Jordan, and Jordan looks at me, to decide who should go first. She nods, signaling for me to take the lead.

"Um, okay," I say to the group, "Hi. I'm Jake."

"And do you have a fun fact about yourself that you'd like to share with us, Jake?" Carolyn asks, still doing the thing where she blinks way too often.

"A fun fact?" I say without really thinking about it first. "No. My life is pretty shitty right now."

Okay, so maybe I should have given that more thought. But whatever. It's the truth. I hear a little bit of laughter from the group, but it's the kind of laughter that makes you wonder if you're a bad person for laughing or not.

"Retweet," Jordan says, pointing her finger up in the air in support.

"Well," Carolyn says, trying to lighten the mood, "you're here. So hopefully the goal is to change that."

Change. *Right.* My life already changed before, but I didn't do anything specific to make it happen. It just sort of happened. I can't will that kind of change into existence.

Carolyn starts to ask Jordan to go next, but Jordan goes ahead and answers before Carolyn even finishes asking the question.

"Yeah," Jordan says with a somehow admirable lack of enthusiasm. "Hey everyone. I'm Jordan. Like she just said. Uh, a fun fact about me is that my parents kicked me out when I was fifteen, and I've been on my own ever since. Oh, and now I'm depressed and bulimic."

Jesus Christ. That's some shit. The room falls completely silent. Even Carolyn isn't sure what to say to that. This "fun fact" game didn't go quite as planned.

"Alright, well," Carolyn says, trying to shift gears. "would anyone like to volunteer to go next?"

I hope the fuck not. That's enough tragic backstory time for today, thank you.

TEN

Tim walks me into his office. There are more books in this room than I've read in my entire life. (I'm not a reader though, so I guess that's not saying much.)

"Go ahead and take a seat wherever you'd like," Tim tells me, as if there are more places to sit than on the couch across from his chair.

He shuts the door and grabs a pen and notepad off his desk.

"So, first day," he says, sitting across from me. "How are meals going?"

Time out, Tim. Can we not make intense eye contact for every second of the next hour please? Jesus.

"Uh, fine," I answer. "It's fine."

I guess that doesn't really answer his question because he follows it up with a question that I assumed was implied in the first one.

"Any issues?" he asks in a way that sounds totally insincere, but I can't exactly pinpoint why.

I know the clinicians tell each other everything. I bet he knows exactly what was in my sandwich at lunch. (Ham, salami, provolone, arugula, and mayo. It was fine, but I could've done without so much bread and like half of the ingredients.)

"Not really," I say honestly. "I hate milk though."

"Any reason?" Tim asks.

"What?" I ask, but what I really mean is *What the hell kind of question is that?*

"Do you have a particular reason for 'hating' milk?" he asks.

"No . . ." I say. "I just don't like how it tastes."

I mean, I hate drinking anything with calories, but even if I didn't, I would still hate milk. It's so bad. I haven't been able to get the horrible taste of it out of my mouth since breakfast.

"Okay," Tim says, but I can't tell if he really believes me or not. "Just checking."

He scribbles a note on his notepad. I feel like to be a therapist you have to know how to write so terribly that it's impossible for anyone else to read your handwriting.

"I'll make sure to let Jessica know," he says. "You'll have your first session with her tomorrow, and you'll be able to talk with her about all of that."

Jessica seems pretty easygoing to me. I can probably talk her into not making me eat or drink certain things, like milk. She looks only a few years older than me, so who knows, maybe she knows who I am and she'll be too starstruck to give me a hard time.

I'm distracted for a solid minute or so by the little clock on Tim's desk. I feel like the ticking sound is way louder to me than it would be to anyone else. I guess Tim notices I'm distracted because he clears his throat and starts speaking a little louder than he was before.

"I think a good place for us to start," he says, "would be to talk about what you hope to get of your time here."

Oh. I see we're not building up to the bigger questions. We're just diving right in instead. Okay. I open my mouth to speak, but no words come out. I mean, what am I supposed to say? I don't know if I want to get anything out of this other than – oh, I don't know – my fucking life back.

"It's okay," Tim says. "Take your time, and be honest."

I take some time to think about how I can put how I feel into words, which definitely isn't my strong suit these days. It's so much easier to just not talk about this shit.

"Honestly, I don't even know," I say. "I feel like a totally different person than I was six months ago."

"Different how?" Tim asks.

"I hate everything now," I say, saying exactly how I feel now without needing to take much time to think about it first. "Things that I used to love, I just don't give a shit about now."

It's quiet after that for a minute as Tim jots some things down on his notepad. I think there's some kind of rule out there that says you're allowed to ask your therapist to show you their notes. I probably won't

39

because I wouldn't be able to read his terrible handwriting anyway.

"Talk to me about the past year or so," Tim says. "How did you go from being who you said you were six months ago to who you are now? What changed?"

"Everything," I say, laughing at the sheer insanity that is my life. "It felt like everything changed. I mean, two years ago, I was in my bedroom singing covers of other people's songs on YouTube . . ."

"And now?" Tim asks.

"Now I'm . . . Jake Parker."

Okay, sure, I've always been Jake Parker, but no one cared who I was before. It's hard to even put into words how much things have changed in that sense.

"You feel like there's pressure on you because of who you are," Tim says.

"I don't just 'feel' like there's pressure," I argue. "There *is* pressure. Pressure to look a certain way, to sound a certain way . . ."

"You have to be perfect."

"I don't even know if it's that I have to be perfect. I think what makes it hard is that I have to be someone all the time. I have to be Jake Parker."

It's quiet again as Tim scribbles some more on his notepad. He clicks the pen in his hand as he thinks for a moment.

I find myself shifting around in my seat a little. I've done so many red carpets and sit-down interviews, but I'm more uncomfortable now than I've ever been doing one of those. Smiling in front of cameras and talking about my music is way easier than talking to someone I just met about how I somehow managed to fall from cloud nine to rock bottom in six months.

"We find that eating disorders usually seem to serve some sort of purpose," Tim explains. "In many cases, it acts as a coping mechanism for something else. Do you have any idea what that might be for you?"

I've never thought about it like that until now, but I immediately know the answer. It's like a bright, LED lightbulb just lit up in my head as soon as he asked the question.

"It's about control," I blurt out. "I mean, there are obviously a lot of things to love about my life, but so much of it feels totally out of my control."

"The eating disorder fulfilled a need for control for you," Tim says, putting my revelation on his back and running with it to the finish line.

"I guess so, yeah," I say, "but I think it ended up making me lose even more control."

Tim nods, and it's like he knew that before I even said it.

"That's exactly what an eating disorder does," he says. "It gives you that illusion of control while actually taking almost all of it away from you."

He gives me a minute to process that. I shit you not, what that man just said is a completely accurate summary of what the last six months of my life have been like.

"The good thing though," Tim goes on, "is that you can regain that control, and it's my job to make sure that that's one of the things you get out of being here."

"Good luck," I say under my breath.

I wish that life had a reset button and I could just do it all again without the eating disorder. That would be so much easier than whatever I'm supposed to do here.

"Well, it's your job as much as it is mine," Tim says. "I know you're motivated, Jake. You wouldn't be as successful as you are if you weren't. So, I think the key for you is to take that motivation and use it to push yourself to get better and to start moving towards recovery. You have to want this as badly as anything you've ever wanted."

ELEVEN

It was around this time last year that I finished recording my first album.

I remember being in the sound booth in the recording studio, just me and my guitar, having the time of my life doing what I loved to do more than anything else in the world. It was amazing honestly.

Aaron Olson came into the recording studio and listened to what we were working on, which was so cool because I've looked up to him since like, forever. He's like me but almost twice my age and more than twice as talented and good-looking as I am. I think basically everyone would agree that he's an exceptionally attractive dude.

"Dude!" Aaron said, taking off his headphones. "This is so good."

"Really?" I say, totally freaking out on the inside but trying to play it cool on the outside.

"Oh yeah," he says. "I couldn't have done what you're doing when I was your age."

There's no way he means that. He's won like three Grammys and has literally had more #1 songs than I've had years on this planet.

"I mean it," he says. "You're so good, man. This is gonna be huge."

I don't know why I didn't believe him because he was totally right. My album *was* huge when it dropped. Like, life-changing huge. It was insane.

It wasn't just one song either. There was a time when if you turned on the radio at any given time, there was a good chance that one of the songs from that album would be playing. I know it sounds like I'm bragging, and maybe I am, but sometimes I still can't believe how fast it all happened.

"If you want to make it, you have to want it," I remember Aaron telling me. "You have to really want it. Not just the music or the fame, you have to want it all. Embrace it and stick with it, and everything else will fall into place. I mean, that's what happened for me, anyway."

Aaron was right about a lot of things, but he wasn't right about how things would pan out from there. I mean, yeah, for a while, it did feel like everything was falling into place . . . but pretty soon it felt like the exact opposite was happening and like everything was starting to fall apart. Including myself.

"But seriously," Aaron said, "hold onto that energy and that passion you have for what you do, and you'll soar, man."

Now, I don't know where that energy and passion went, and I'm honestly not convinced I'll ever get it back. So much for soaring.

Two weeks before the album came out, I did my first-ever photoshoot for a popular magazine. I was sitting on a stool in front of huge, bright lights and a swarm of people. I was so out of my element then, but I didn't really feel nervous at first. I actually felt good – confident, even. That's something I haven't felt in a while.

At one point, the photographer, an eccentric little woman with a thick French accent, put her camera down to look through the photos she'd taken of me so far. I couldn't see what was on the screen, but I could sense that whatever it was wasn't good.

The photographer turned to one of the make-up artists in the room and motioned for her to come see what she was looking at on the camera. I've never been the anxious type, but I was beyond uncomfortable as they were looking at those photos.

What did they see that was so bad? My mind immediately jumped to FAT. Of course. That's what must have been wrong with the photos, and that's what must have been wrong with me.

I remember making eye contact with Cat, who was across the room behind the lights and everything, and she could instantly tell that something was wrong. That's how well she knows me. She quickly moved over to where the photographer and make-up artist were standing to see what the hell was happening.

"Is there a problem?" Cat asked with a seemingly polite but definitely passive-aggressive smile.

The photographer was so caught off-guard by Cat approaching her like that. In hindsight, it was kind of funny, but I didn't think so in the moment because of the all the other shit going on in my head.

I think what made it all worse is that I'd already lost a few pounds. I thought maybe it wasn't enough. Maybe I needed to cut back more.

"There's just a little bit of. . ." the make-up artist tried to explain to Cat on the photographer's behalf.

"Acne?" Cat shot back. "Yeah, he's eighteen. Teenagers have acne."

Okay, so maybe it wasn't fat. I don't know if that made me feel any better though. I couldn't silence the voice in my head that was telling that I needed to lose weight and that that's what would make me feel better – it would make me feel more in control. I couldn't control when my face would break out, but my weight was something I could control.

I'll just lose a few more pounds, I thought. *I'll look better, and if I look better, I'll feel better. Just a few more pounds. I'm completely in control. I'm fine.*

If I didn't tell myself that, I wouldn't have had the confidence I needed to get through the rest of the shoot. I wouldn't have been able to smile and look so comfortable if I didn't feel like I had control over something and like I could actually do something to feel better about myself and everything that was going on around me.

46

"He's a good-looking kid," Cat said to the photographer. "Just take the damn photo."

TWELVE

I'm making breakfast on my second day at Path. I slide a plate with two frozen sausage patties on it into the microwave and set the timer for two minutes.

I think about what Cat would say about me eating frozen meat. Probably something about fat and preservatives. Whatever. I used to eat this kind of shit as a kid all the time actually. Whenever my mom was too hungover to make breakfast, Jimmy Dean had our back with his world-class frozen breakfast sandwiches. (Shout out to my friends at Kellogg's, too, for making Pop-Tarts. I'm trash for cookies & cream anything, and cookies & cream Pop-Tarts are probably better than sex.)

I look inside my brown paper bag to see what else I have to eat for breakfast. I don't see milk, which is definitely a relief. I have a yogurt, a cheese stick, and a juice box. I'm a little annoyed about the juice because I don't like to drink calories and juice isn't all that good for you anyway because it's more sugar than it is fruit, but fuck it – I'll drink it. It's apple juice, so even if it has little to no nutritional value, at least I know I won't hate it.

Jordan picks out the plastic-wrapped cheese stick from her bag.

"The fuck is this?" she asks, looking at it like it's the most disgusting thing she's ever laid eyes on.

"Cheese?" I say, not seeing the problem.

48

"This . . ." Jordan says, wiggling the highly processed cheese stick around in the air, "is *not* cheese."

"It's better than milk," I say, taking my plate out of the microwave.

"Huh," Jordan says with more than a hint of salt, "Someone's in a better mood today."

Believe me, I hate being here as much as Jordan does. Maybe even more given my circumstances and everything I had to leave behind for this. I just don't feel like making a big deal about having to eat frozen sausage or a fucking cheese stick.

During breakfast, Lily asks how me and Jordan are "adjusting." It takes us a minute to realize she's talking to us, probably because we've been actively trying to avoid her.

"Uh, it's going okay I guess," I say, shrugging. "Day one was kinda rough."

"Yeah, it always is," Lily says. "My first day was rough, too. My whole first week here was hard."

Why does it feel like we're inmates comparing each other's experiences in captivity? Huh. There are probably some valid comparisons to be made there. I'm not loving the food here so far, but I can't imagine it's worse than whatever the hell they serve in prison.

49

"My whole first month here was hell," Morgan, definitely the weirdest girl here, says.

I can't figure out what Morgan's deal is, and that frustrates the hell out of me for some reason. She's overweight – like, super overweight – and looks younger than everyone else, but it's hard to tell her age. How old is she? Does she even have an eating disorder? Binge-eating maybe. Whatever.

"Shit," Jordan says. "How long have you been here?"

"Since I was thirteen," Morgan says, "so three years."

Jordan is so shocked that she almost chokes on her food. I probably shouldn't find that funny, but I do.

"THREE YEARS?" Jordan says, raising her voice like ten decibels over where it was before.

Samantha clears her throat and glances at Jordan. She doesn't say anything, but her expression says it all.

"Sorry," Jordan says, quieter and looking a little embarrassed now.

"It's okay," Morgan says, which is surprisingly mature for someone like her. "This is my third time in residential. Hopefully my last."

She randomly starts crying, so I guess I'll take back the comment about her being mature. Jesus. Get your shit together, Morgan.

I can't even wrap my head around the fact that's she been doing this treatment bullshit for three years. Three years. I mean, three years ago I was a sophomore at a public high school in Seattle. That feels like such a long time ago to me. I can't imagine being here for that long. Today's only my second day, and I already can't wait to get the hell out of here and get back to my life.

Jordan takes the tiniest bite out of her cheese stick. She glances at me as I'm figuratively digging myself deep into a dark, existential hole of thinking.

"Jake," she says, nudging me in the shoulder to snap me back into it. "You okay?"

I nod. I mean, I'm not okay obviously, but like, compared to someone who's been doing this for three years, I guess I could be doing a lot worse. There's no way in hell I'm staying here for three years . . . Right?

THIRTEEN

Jessica walks me into her office, which is small compared to Tim's, but I think I like it more. It's neat and organized, and it's better decorated than Tim's office. I mean, it's a little too chic for my taste, but it works for Jessica. Her whole aesthetic is like everything was ripped right off a Pinterest board, and her office is the same way.

"Make yourself comfortable," Jessica says, and I take a seat on the couch (which is rose gold, of course).

Instead of sitting at her desk or in the chair across from mine, Jessica sits right next to me on the couch. She sits with her legs crossed and looks so relaxed that I can almost forget that I'm talking to a "clinician" and not one of my friends.

"So, I have your meal plan in here," Jessica says, showing me a green folder, "and there's a guide in there that sort of explains the method behind it, but basically, your meal plan is designed to make sure you restore weight at a healthy pace."

I hate when people say they're "triggered" by something, but I'm internally freaking the fuck out as soon as Jessica starts talking about gaining weight. I know that's basically why I'm here, but I hate thinking about this as a reverse fat camp or something.

"How much weight are we talking here?" I ask, trying to stay calm and not completely lose my shit.

"Well . . ." Jessica says, and she takes a second to think about it before going on. "Let me ask you this. Understanding that you're going to have to gain some weight, how much weight would you feel comfortable with gaining? If any."

Ha. Ha. Ha. None. I don't want to gain weight. I know I can't say that to Jessica though.

"I mean, like five or six pounds would be fine," I say, hoping I'm in the right ballpark because I can't imagine gaining much more weight than that.

"Okay, so you're willing to gain some weight," Jessica says. "That's something."

If I had to guess based on the way she said that, we're not in the same ballpark. Fuck. How much weight does she think I need to gain? I'll be damned if my jeans don't fit when I get out of here.

"Why don't we make it a goal for you not to think about numbers?" Jessica asks.

Okay, I see what she's doing. Dancing right around my question and basically telling me to forget about it. Whatever.

"Numbers?" I ask, but I'm pretty sure I already know what she means.

"Knowing your weight, counting calories . . ." she explains. "I'll take care of all of that for you now."

She smiles at me as if she just told me the best fucking news of my life instead of the exact opposite. I'm honestly surprised that I don't hate her. I don't know why, and it kind of frustrates me because if I did hate her, I would be able to stand up for myself more.

"*Great*," I say sarcastically, because I can't bring myself to say anything else and can't really put into words how I feel right now.

There's no control for me without numbers. I'm not in control if I don't know how much I weigh and if I don't know how many calories are in literally everything that goes into my body. Like, "How many calories are in toothpaste?" is something you might come across if you were to look through my Google search history. I wish I were joking.

"Hey, I know this is hard," Jessica says, putting her hand on my knee, "but you're here and you're doing it, and that's more than a lot of people can say, right?"

"I guess so," I say, although comparing me to people who are worse off isn't exactly motivating for me.

"This is totally doable, Jake," Jessica assures me. "I promise."

FOURTEEN

"For those of you who are newer," Carolyn says, glancing towards me and Jordan in the group room, "we use this time every day to talk about anything we're feeling or struggling with that we want to talk about with the group."

I notice that Jordan isn't paying attention at all. She's too focused on whatever she's drawing in her notebook and totally tuning out her surroundings.

"Let's start today by naming at least one emotion to describe how we're feeling, and that should give us a feel for the energy of the group," Carolyn explains like a teacher going over the rules for a dumb game that no one wants to play. "Who can start us off?"

"I can," Lauren says, passively throwing up her hand with no enthusiasm.

"Go ahead," Carolyn tells her with a smile.

"Apathetic," Lauren says.

I'll be honest and say that I only vaguely know what that word means. Carolyn seems to know though because she nods and writes it down on her notepad.

"I feel really happy!" Lily says excitedly, but then her expression changes to a frown in a split second. "But also kinda sad."

I don't even know what to say about this bitch anymore. She still annoys the hell out of me though.

"Ooookay," Carolyn says, raising an eyebrow, "that is totally valid, Lily."

It's probably some kind of rule here that you have to tell people their emotions are valid even if they're stupid. I don't know productive that is, but whatever.

Tori, one of the clients I haven't interacted with much, speaks up next. She's probably around my mom's age, but she looks better than my mom does because my mom is an alcoholic and a chainsmoker. Tori looks . . . normal, actually. She's by no means fat, but she doesn't look underweight to me.

"I'm feeling sad today," Tori says, "I'm really disappointed in myself."

She tries to hold back tears but ends up crying anyway. Lauren hands her a box of tissues.

Morgan is up next. If you think Tori is an exception to stereotypes, Morgan is the polar opposite of what you'd think someone with an eating disorder looks like. I feel bad for the dietitians because it's like pulling teeth to get her to finish her food at meals, but it's so bizarre to me because clearly this girl eats. Maybe she keeps a stash of junk food in her room or something and overeating is her problem. Is that even an eating disorder though? Whatever.

"I feel hopeless," Morgan says, staring at the floor to avoid eye contact with everyone looking at her.

"Is there anything you want to add to that?" Carolyn asks, and Morgan just shakes her head no.

"Okay," Carolyn says, "Let us know if there's anything we can do to help."

Carolyn turns to me and Jordan now, and as usual, I take the lead.

"I don't know," I say. "I don't know how the hell I ended up here."

I snicker and shake my head.

I shouldn't be here.

I should be in L.A. with Cat and Aaron and the rest of the Jake Parker entourage getting ready to go on tour.

I shouldn't be here.

Jordan seems to feel the same way, but I don't know what her life was like before this. I can't imagine it was anything mine was.

"I feel numb," Jordan says to the group. "Depressed, too. But like, that's always."

Carolyn nods and writes down Jordan's response.

I look over at what Jordan's drawing in her notebook, and I immediately regret it. I see a drawing of a naked girl being strangled by thick, thorny vines colored in thoroughly with black marker. The girl in the drawing looks enough like Jordan for me to assume that it's her . . . but the girl in the drawing is fatter. Like, a lot fatter. The

57

vines are wrapped so tight around her body that pockets of fat bulge out in sections, most noticeably around her stomach.

Jordan catches me looking at her drawing, and I quickly look away, but now I can't get that image out of my head. It's dark, depressing, and really fucking disturbing. Maybe Jordan is in a worse place than I thought, which bums me out because I care about her. I know we haven't known each other for very long, but I feel closer to her than I have to anyone this all started.

"Okay, well, the floor is now open to the group," Carolyn says, flipping over to a new page in her notepad.

Lauren doesn't wait even a second to call out Tori, who's still dabbing her eyes with a tissue after crying.

"Tori, what's up," Lauren says. "Talk to us."

"Okay," Tori says, and she takes a moment to pull herself together. "I talked to my daughter last night, and she asked when I'm coming home. She's five."

Damn. That's gotta be hard.

"I should be home," Tori goes on. "I should be taking my daughter to school every day and cooking dinner for her every night. But I'm here, and I feel like I'm failing as a parent."

"I get that," Lauren says, even though she's like, my age, and not a mom as far as I know, so she doesn't *really* get it, "but like, you're taking care of yourself. You're making yourself better every day just by being here."

"Your daughter isn't old enough to understand now," Carolyn adds, "but when she's older she'll know that you needed to take time to put your health first and that you were able to be a better mom because of it."

So, yeah, maybe Tori isn't a perfect parent, but like, who is? My mom's way more of a mess than Tori is, but Tori's owning it and doing something about it, and that's a step that my mom might never take.

"My parents don't get it," Morgan says. "They don't even seem to care anymore."

"Yeah, same," Lauren agrees.

I see I'm not the only one with problematic parents. I guess that's not too surprising though. *These things don't just come from nowhere, Sarah.*

"Well, recovery is hard for everyone, right?" Carolyn says. "Not just for us but for the people who care about us, too. It's a process, and it can be really hard."

"Yeah," Morgan says in a way that also means *tell me about it.*

"Jake, I'm curious to know what that's been like for you given your situation," Carolyn says, putting me on the spot.

(My 'situation' meaning the fact that I'm famous and only a handful of people know where I am right now.)

"What does your support system look like?" Carolyn asks me.

"That's code for tell us which celebrities you're tight with," Lauren adds, and Carolyn just shoots her a look that says *Now's not the time.*

Lauren apologizes, but it's not like she said anything wrong. If anything, I appreciate the comedic relief from this group therapy bullshit.

"No, it's cool," I say. "Um . . . I don't know. I don't know if I have much of a support system."

"What about your parents?" Tori asks me.

"They're divorced," I explain. "I don't have a great relationship with either of them, and they live in Seattle, so they haven't really been a part of this."

I notice that Jordan stops drawing when I start talking about my parents. I guess she can relate.

"So it's all on you then," Tori says, coming to the same terrifying realization that's been hanging over me since I got here.

"Yeah, pretty much," I say, and it's like I can see Tori's heart breaking in real time. "I have a handful of people who actually care, but my parents have their own shit to worry about."

I make eye contact with Jordan, and I swear it's like the world stops spinning just for us and this moment. We don't say anything to each other, and we don't need to, because I feel like I know so much about her just by looking at her now . . .

Is it weird that I'm kind of rooting for her more than I am for myself at this point?

FIFTEEN

"Talk to me about your parents," Tim says in our next session. "What's your relationship with them like?"

"Complicated," I say, "to say the least."

"Let's start with your mom," Tim says. "How do you get along with her?"

"Fine," I shrug. "I mean, she's an alcoholic, and I worry about her a lot, but we get along for the most part. Sometimes I just wish that she took more care of herself."

"And what about your dad?"

"He used to be the one with a drinking problem. Now he just works all the time, and that's all he really cares about anymore."

"Has it been difficult for you to be away from home?" Tim asks. "From Seattle, I mean?"

"I don't think so," I say honestly. "I think it's better that way."

"You like the independence."

"I just feel like it's easier for me to be away from all the family bullshit."

"Easier," Tim echoes, and he scribbles the word onto his notepad.

I mean, yeah, it's easier being away from my parents. I don't have to worry about my mom being too drunk to find her way home, and I don't have to pretend like my dad not having time for me doesn't bother me. I don't know if they realize how hard that was for me.

"You have a younger sister," Tim says, looking through his notes to find her name. "Jule. Does she still live at home?"

"Yeah," I say. "She's thirteen. She lives with my mom. She used to see my dad on weekends, and then every other weekend, and now just it's whenever he feels like making time to see her."

As we're talking about Jule, I start to wonder if I'm selfish for leaving her with our batshit crazy parents.

"Does she know you're here?"

"Probably. I don't know. I haven't talked to her."

I can't talk to Jule now. I don't even know what I would say to her.

Oh, hey Jule. I hate to tell you this, but I majorly fucked up, and now I'm in treatment for an eating disorder.

Jule wouldn't say 'I told you so.' I'm not worried about that. I just don't want her to worry about me. She's like I am (or used to be) because she cares too much about people. She has enough on her plate with just my parents. I don't want to add to that. I'm not worth it.

"You're pretty hard on yourself, aren't you?" Tim points out.

"I guess," I say.

63

Of course I'm hard on myself. I have to be. That was basically in the fine print when I signed up to be in the spotlight.

"If your sister were sick and she needed to go to treatment to get better, would you talk about her the way you talk about yourself?" Tim asks me.

Damn. I should've known that's where he was going with this. I feel like that warrants a slow clap, but I resist the temptation to be a smart-ass.

"Of course not," I say, a little annoyed by how smoothly Tim can segue into whatever he wants to tell me.

"Why not?" he asks.

"Because she's my sister," I say, which I'm sure is exactly what Tim expects me to say.

"Because she's not Jake Parker," Tim says. "No matter how talented or how successful you are, Jake, you're still human. If you keep holding yourself to these impossible standards, you'll just keep hurting yourself in the long run."

"I'm already hurting myself," I say, shaking my head.

This is isn't a bad pep talk, but it's more than a day late and a dollar short. It's like, six months late and a cancelled world tour short. It's too late for this shit.

"Why are you here then?" Tim asks. "Aren't you here to get better?"

"Sure, but so is everyone else," I argue. "That doesn't mean I *will* get better. Morgan's been doing this for three years. Three years. You think she just doesn't want to get better?"

"I honestly don't know," Tim admits. "I won't speak for her."

I feel a little proud of myself for winning that one, but it's a stupid sense of pride that doesn't even compare to how pathetic I feel right now. It was so much easier when I didn't talk about my eating disorder with anyone because I could pretend like it wasn't even a thing. Now it's like I'm coming face to face with the worst part of myself every fucking day of my life.

"There's something we refer to in recovery as The Rule of Thirds," Tim says. "Do you know about it?"

I shake my head no.

"It's not exact," Tim explains, "but we say that about one third of people with an eating disorder never recover. So you're right, not everyone recovers. The next third gets part of the way there. And only the last third makes a full recovery."

The worst thing about my sessions with Tim is that for every pep talk, there's a depressing reality check, and I never know when either is coming.

"What do you think it is about the people in the last group that sets them apart from the others?" Tim asks as if there can be even be a real answer to a question like that.

"I don't know," I shrug. "Luck? Genetics?"

Tim shakes his head no.

"It's an incredible amount of strength and motivation," Tim explains, "and you can only find it within yourself."

Yeah, that's a bullshit answer.

"I don't have that," I say. "And if I ever did, I don't have it now."

"It'll take some time and a lot of hard work to find it, but you can do it, Jake," Tim insists. "I have no doubt about it."

SIXTEEN

I remember how I felt when I performed at that award show six months ago. It was so cool to perform in front of thousands of people who all knew the words to my song.

It was so cool to come backstage after the show see Cat and Aaron there waiting for me. They looked prouder of me than my parents ever have.

"I'm so proud of you," Cat said, hugging me. "That song will be back at #1 on iTunes tomorrow."

"You killed it out there," Aaron said to me with a handshake that evolved into a bro-hug. "You're killin' it, man."

"Thanks," I said, putting my guitar aside.

"So, I made a reservation at the Four Seasons in Beverly Hills for tonight," Cat said to me, looking at the jam-packed calendar on her phone.

"For what?" I asked.

"Some executives from the label want to meet over dinner to talk about the next album," Cat explained. "If all goes well, we could have a contract by Monday, like I said when we talked about it *last* Monday."

Hmm. Nope. That didn't ring a bell. I love Cat, but she tells me too much shit to remember it all. I'm glad I have her to keep up with everything though because I sure as hell couldn't do it on my own.

"Wow," I said. "That's awesome, Cat."

"I know," she said. "The chef there makes the best tiramisu on the West Coast."

WHAT.

"Tiramisu?"

"Oh, relax," Cat said, still doing things on her phone as she talks to me. "You don't have to eat it. It goes well with prosecco . . ."

She looks up from her phone for a second to emphasize her next words, pointing a finger at me every time she says the word 'you.'

". . . which *you* will not be drinking because *you* are underage."

"Mmhmm," I mumbled sarcastically, even though I probably wouldn't drink even if I could.

"Mmhmm," Cat said back, shifting her attention back to whatever she was doing on her phone.

"What am I gonna eat?" I asked, because God knows I'm not eating tiramisu.

"I don't know," Cat said. "We'll order you a pizza or something. Teenagers like pizza, right?"

"I don't want pizza," I snapped back, sounding way more aggressive than I meant to sound.

Of course I like pizza. That doesn't mean I eat it. Besides, I felt like I'd eaten too much that day already, and pizza would just make me feel worse about myself.

I could tell that Cat was really frustrated with me because she put her phone away and put her hands on my shoulders.

"Jake, I love you, but you're being difficult," she said, looking me in the eyes. "It's just food. We have bigger things to worry about than what you're eating. Okay?"

I nodded. *It's just food.*

The conversation I had with Cat that night came up again before the photoshoot I talked about earlier.

I was in my dressing room getting ready with Cat hovering over me as always. There were some other people in the room, too, but they kept their distance from Cat, as I notice people tend to do.

Cat tugged at the waist of my pants as I finished buttoning up my shirt in front of the mirror.

"Why do your pants look so big?" she asked.

"I don't know," I said, shrugging. "Maybe I lost weight?"

There was no 'maybe' about it, though. I'd already lost some weight, but I didn't want to talk about it. *It's just a few pounds*, I thought. *No one has to know.*

Something you should know about Cat though is that she takes a lot of pride in her ability to call people out on their bullshit, so of course she wouldn't let it go. She knew better.

"The wardrobe fitting was two weeks ago," Cat said, and she tugged on my waist again to prove her point. "How could you have lost this much weight since then without knowing?"

I basically lost it after she said that. I respected Cat, and I still do, but sometimes I feel like sometshe has no respect for boundaries. It's never been in her job description to harass me about my weight.

"I don't know, Cat!" I yelled, throwing my hands up furiously. "And I don't care. Don't you think we have bigger things to worry about?"

I wish I hadn't said that. I could tell that it hurt her, but I was too upset in the moment to care. I stormed past her and bolted out of the room, letting the door slam shut behind me. I think that's when Cat started to realize what was going on with me, because she didn't look at me the same after that.

After that, Cat started looking at me like you look at someone on their deathbed who's too sick to even know they're dying. I wasn't dying, but I honestly wouldn't have cared even if I were.

SEVENTEEN

We're eating dinner one night, and towards the end of the meal, Lauren finally asks what I know she's been waiting to ask since I got here.

"Okay, Jake, I need to know this," Lauren says very seriously. "Who is the most famous person you know."

"I met Taylor Swift once," I say casually.

"You're shitting me," Lauren says, freaking out. "Did you sing with her? Or did you like . . . ?"

"No, definitely not what you're thinking," I say, laughing.

I love Taylor Swift as much as anyone, but she's way out of my league and like a decade older than me.

"I just bumped into her at an after party once," I explain. "She was cool."

She *was* cool! I wasn't even that famous when I met her, but she already knew who I was, which was insane. Oh, and we added each other on Snapchat afterwards. We haven't talked since then, but yeah, she's cool.

I get distracted for a second because Samantha gets up from the table and walks over to the freezer. She puts a pint of ice cream out on the counter.

God, I love ice cream. I haven't eaten it in a while for obvious reasons, but there was a time when I seriously considered going on an all ice cream diet.

71

"Who's the most famous person you're tight with?" Lauren asks me.

"Probably Aaron Olson," I say.

Definitely Aaron Olson. I'm closer to him than I am to anyone besides Cat.

"Ugh, what a man," Lauren says.

I can't help but laugh at how unapologetically thirsty this girl is. I don't blame her though.

"He looks even better in person," I say.

"Dude, I'm so jealous," Lauren says. "Like, I want your life."

Ha. Ha. Ha. I don't think she does.

"You can have it," I say, jokingly throwing my napkin down in surrender. "It's cool, but it's a lot, trust me."

There's so much that comes with being famous that no one tells you about . . . and if they do, you try to tune them out because you don't want to think about it.

Samantha brings a bowl of ice cream over to Jordan. She sets it in front of Jordan without saying anything and goes back to her seat at the table.

I see Jordan staring the ice cream down hard. She looks terrified of it.

"Is that a challenge food?" I ask her in a whisper, pointing to the bowl.

"Yep," Jordan confirms. "Fuck me."

"No thanks," I say, hoping to lighten the mood a little with my world-class sarcasm.

"You know what I mean," Jordan says, unamused.

'Challenge foods' are pretty much what they sound like. They tend to be foods like cake and cookies that our eating disorders don't want us to eat, so by eating those foods here, we're learning how to "challenge" the eating disorder I guess.

"Is that cookies & cream?" I ask, squinting as I try to read the packaging on the pint on the counter from where I'm sitting.

"I don't care what flavor it is," Jordan says. "It's just fat and calories to me."

Excuse me. Don't you dare disrespect cookies & cream like that. I take a second to think before I make my next move.

"Uh, Jessica?" I say. "Can I have ice cream?"

Jessica looks as surprised as you are that I'm actually *asking* for ice cream. She almost chokes on her food.

"Um, yeah," she says after taking a second to pull herself together. "Yeah, of course."

Everyone's looking at me now, and I can feel my face turning red, but whatever. I asked for ice cream, and there's no turning back now.

73

"What are you doing?" Jordan hisses.

"I'm having ice cream," I say, shrugging, "and so are you."

"It's not part of your meal plan," Jordan says.

"And that's okay," I say, even though there's still a part of me that says it isn't. "I want to have ice cream with you, so I'm gonna have ice cream."

"You're insane," Jordan says.

"Probably," I admit, shrugging.

Jessica brings a bowl of ice cream over and sets it in front of me.

It's not like I suddenly don't have an eating disorder. That part of me is still there, and it's taking everything I have to ignore what it's telling me. I'm not even doing it just because I want ice cream. I'm doing it because I want my life back. *It's just food*, I tell myself until I start to believe it, even if it's just for now.

I dig my spoon into the ice cream and eat a spoonful of it without giving my eating disorder time to change its mind.

Holy shit. It tastes even better than I thought it would. Jordan's not wrong about the fat and calories, but this might just be worth it. I might have to reconsider that all ice cream diet idea.

"Your turn," I say, nodding to Jordan.

"So what?" Jordan asks. "We're just gonna go back and forth all night eating ice cream by the spoonful?"

"Why not?" I ask. "We don't have anything better to do."

"You're insane," Jordan says, shaking her head.

She just goes for it and eats a whole spoonful of ice cream, and I can't help but smile because I'm so damn proud of her.

"You're a badass," I tell her.

Jordan smiles, too, and I realize that I've never seen her smile like this before. It's pretty cool to see.

"You think I'm a badass?" Jordan asks.

"Totally," I say, and I eat another spoonful of victory over my eating disorder.

EIGHTEEN

I'm in my room at Path. I know it's late, but I've been too busy writing to keep track of the time.

My cell phone vibrates, and I stop writing for a second to check it. It's 2 A.M., and I haven't slept even though I know we have to wake up early tomorrow for weigh-in.

There's a Twitter notification below the time on my lock screen. I see a tweet from one of those stupid tabloid accounts.

Where is @JakeParkerMusic? Here Are Our 10 Craziest Theories!

Whatever. I know this is the last place anyone would expect me to be. I'm not too concerned with whatever crazy Jake Parker theories are right now. People can think whatever they want about where I am, and Cat will figure out how to explain it later. I swipe the notification away and go back to what I was doing.

I hear a quiet knock on my door. *Who the hell is at my door this late at night?* I decide to ignore it. I'm so tired that I don't rule out the possibility that I'm just hearing things.

I hear a knock again, so I put aside what I'm doing and finally get up to see who's at the door.

I open the door, and I see Jordan standing there in her pajamas. Of course. Who else would be awake at 2

A.M. on a Sunday night? I don't think I'd be shocked if I found out she doesn't sleep at all.

"Heeey," Jordan says super casually.

"What are you doing here?" I ask, trying to keep my voice low so I don't wake anyone up. "It's like, two in the morning."

"I couldn't sleep," Jordan shrugs. "I saw your light was on, so I thought I'd come check on you – you know, just to make sure you're okay."

"That's thoughtful of you . . ." I say, raising an eyebrow. "Suspicious, even."

I glance down at her pajama pants, which I don't think I've had the pleasure of seeing before.

"Power Rangers," I say with a teasing smile. "Interesting choice."

"Still think I'm a badass?" Jordan asks.

"Less so," I admit, "but yes."

"Great," she says. "Now let me in."

"Fine," I say, opening the door for her to come in.

She comes in and sits on my bed, immediately making herself comfortable. Something's off about her.

"I think I know why you can't sleep . . ." I say, quietly shutting the door. "You're nervous about weigh-in tomorrow."

"I mean, yeah," Jordan says. "Aren't you?"

I shrug and sit next to her on the bed.

"I know I've gained weight since I've been here," I say. "I can tell."

"And you're okay with that?" Jordan asks.

"No," I say, "but I want to be okay with it."

Okay, wait. Time-out. Can we talk about how awesome I sounded just now? Tim would be proud.

"They won't tell us the number anyway," I say. "Gaining weight is just part of being here. We hate it, and we're doing it anyway."

"It sucks," Jordan says.

It does. I nod, and she rests her head on my shoulder for a little while as we think about how tired we are and how the hell we're gonna make it through weigh-in tomorrow without totally falling apart.

Jordan picks up my leather-bound journal from the bed.

"Is this your diary?" she asks, teasingly waving it up in the air.

"No," I say, taking it from her. "It's where I write my music."

"Oh," Jordan says, disappointed. "That's not as cool as Jake Parker's secret diary would have been."

78

"It's sort of like a diary," I say, thumbing through pages of messy, handwritten lyrics to songs I might never get to perform. "That's what's so cool about music. You can pull from real life and write about anything."

"What were you writing about just now?" Jordan asks.

"What makes you think I was writing?" I shoot back, and she just gives me a look that tells me to cut the crap.

"Okay, so I *was* writing," I admit. "It's probably not your kind of music though."

Jordan rolls her eyes.

"Right, because all a girl with dyed hair and dark eyeliner listens to is Panic! at the Disco," she says.

"That's not what I'm saying," I insist, even though that's basically what I'm saying

"Let me hear it then," Jordan says. "At least a little bit. Come on."

"Alright, fine," I give in. "Just . . . don't pretend to like it just to be nice, okay? Tell me what you really think."

"When have you ever known me to say something just to be nice?" Jordan asks, and I guess I can't argue with that.

"Fair point," I say.

I flip through my journal to the song I started writing tonight, and I can't believe I'm about to do this. Why am I more afraid to sing in front of Jordan than I was to sing in front of thousands of people? Where the hell did that confidence go?

I take a deep breath, and I do it. I sing something that until now, has only existed in my head and on the pages of my journal. It's not finished, but there's enough there to give her the gist of it.

I've never written anything like it before. That's not to say that my older music isn't good – it's just not as personal as what I'm writing now. I totally meant it when I said it's like a diary. I guess that's what makes it so hard to share now.

I feel so awkward and self-conscious when I finish singing that song for the first time. I close my journal and glance up at Jordan.

"That's all I have so far," I say, and I'm like, embarrassed about how embarrassed I am right now, if that even makes sense.

Hi, I'm Jake Parker, and I get nervous singing in front of my best friend.

Okay, wait. Time-out again. Is Jordan my best friend? Is it weird for me to say that? Am I *her* best friend, too? I don't know why I care so much about what Jordan thinks of me, but I'd be lying if I said that I didn't.

"You hate it, don't you?" I ask her, and I'm pretty sure that she does.

"No, I don't hate it," she says. "I mean, you're no Brendon Urie, but you're pretty good I guess."

I don't exactly aspire to be like Brendon Urie, so I'm okay with that. I'm relieved that she didn't hate it though. I know she just said that I'm "pretty good," but it's as hard to get a genuine compliment out of Jordan as it is to get a #1 song on iTunes.

I feel like we're having a moment here, and I don't know why I'm surprised by what happens next because I totally should have felt it coming.

Jordan leans in to kiss me in the spur of the moment. Oh my god. She's kissing me. This is really happening.

I pull away from her all of a sudden and spring up from the bed.

"I'm so sorry," I say, even more embarrassed now than I was before.

"Oh. My. God," Jordan says as she seems to figure out what's going on here.

"What?" I ask because maybe she doesn't know what I think she knows.

"Are you gay?" she asks.

Okay, so she knows. I guess there's no point in denying it now. I just nod and smile like the embarrassed idiot I am.

"Fuck," Jordan says, letting herself fall back onto the bed. "I had a feeling."

We start laughing because what else would we do in a situation like this?

"Don't tell anyone," I say, still smiling but trying to be serious, "Please."

"I won't, I won't," Jordan says, sitting up, "but you should."

"No way," I say.

I don't want everyone to know that I have an eating disorder, and I sure as hell don't want them to know that I'm gay. I don't know which one would be worse for my career, and I don't want to find out.

"Do you even look at Twitter?" Jordan asks. "You're not even out, and the gays already love you."

I haven't come out because I know it'll totally change how people see me. I want people to know me for my music, not for being gay. I don't know why being gay should matter any more than being straight, but I guess that's besides the point. Jordan seems to have a totally different vision for my future based on what she says next.

"Dude, you could be, like, in the Gay Holy Trinity," she says. "Oh my god. Lady Gaga, Elton John, and Jake Parker."

Yeah, no thanks. I don't know if that's for me. Maybe I'll run that idea by Cat sometime just to hear her tell me how batshit crazy it is.

"Ugh, whatever," Jordan says, and we laugh again.

"I love you," I say, and it's like I'm surprised by my own words because I didn't even think about it first.

"But like, platonically," Jordan adds.

"Right," I say. "Platonically."

I guess we are best friends then, or something like that. Cool. I catch myself smiling like an idiot again thinking about it.

"I should probably go," Jordan says, getting up from the bed. "Um, sorry . . . about this."

"Don't even worry about it," I say, because honestly, it's been a long time since I felt as close to someone as I did to Jordan just now.

"Cool," Jordan says with a smile, starting to sound more like me.

I open the door for her, and she steps out into the hall.

"Good night," I say quietly as she starts to walk back to her room.

Jordan turns to look at me and smiles.

"Good night, Jake," she says.

NINETEEN

It's the morning after the most awkward kiss of my life, and I'm standing with Jordan in line for weigh-in at 7 A.M. They make us wear these stupid hospital gowns, but I'm way too tired to complain about it. Ugh.

Morgan comes out of the room where we do weigh-in, and homegirl is a mess. Her face is blood red, and it's obvious that she's been crying. I try to smile at her, but she brushes past us without making eye contact. I still don't know what her deal is, but I feel for her. She might have different problems that I have, but I know this isn't easy for any of us.

I wish Jordan didn't see that because it seems to make her even more anxious about weigh-in than she already was.

Tori goes in, which makes Jordan next in line. I've never seen Jordan like this. She's shaking and can't stand still. I'm worried she's about to have an anxiety attack or something. I grab her hand and squeeze as if I can somehow squeeze some of the anxiety out of her.

"You can do this," I say, still squeezing her hand. "You're a badass, remember?"

Jordan laughs a little and jokingly shoves me in the chest.

"You're so stupid," she says.

"I'm okay with that," I say with a smile.

Tori comes out and half-smiles at us, but it's the kind of smile you have when you want to smile but you're deep down you're sad and the situation doesn't call for one.

It's Jordan's turn now. I see her take a deep breath, and she nods her head.

"I'm a badass," she whispers, with all the confidence she needs to walk through that door.

She walks into the room for weigh-in, and not only am I smiling like an idiot again, but I feel like I might cry, too. I sort of hate myself for almost getting emotional, but fuck it. I'm so proud of her.

TWENTY

"So, you're almost at the end of week three . . ." Tim says in our session on Thursday of that week. "How are you feeling?"

I could lie and tell you that time is just flying by here, but I'll be honest – it hasn't been terrible, but I swear it feels like time moves slower here. Every day feels the same, and I'm at the point now where I've already tried all the different food options they have here.

Everything's going okay though. I'm following my meal plan and haven't caused any problems. Jessica lets me drink chocolate soy milk instead of regular white milk, and I get to have ice cream every night, so it's cool.

"I feel pretty good," I say, and I mean it.

There's still that part of me that wants to know how much I weigh and exactly how many calories I'm taking in, but I've gotten a lot better at recognizing it and fighting it. It's a hell of a fight, and I don't always win, but I'll never get out of here if I don't keep trying.

"I have to say, Jake, that I'm truly impressed by the progress you're making," Tim says. "I know it's not easy, but it's been incredible to watch you grow.

"Literally," I say, hinting at however much weight I've gained in just the past three weeks.

It's probably for the best that they don't tell us how much we weigh while we're here. I think about it a lot, but

I know I would think about it even more if I actually knew my weight.

"You're putting in the work now," Tim says, "and it shows. The progress you've made in three weeks is more than I've seen a lot of people make in six. You should be really proud of that."

"Thanks," I say, and Tim walks over to his desk to pick up some paperwork.

"So, having said that," he says, grabbing a pen, "I have some paperwork here for you to sign to be discharged."

WHAT.

"Discharged?" I say in total disbelief.

"Assuming that you stay on track in your recovery and continue to restore weight after you leave here," Tim says, "I'd feel very comfortable letting you go after next week. If you think you're ready."

Before I know it, I'm like, sobbing uncontrollably. I guess I don't know how else to react. I wasn't prepared for this at all.

Tim hands me the discharge paperwork, and seeing it makes me want to cry even more. Jake Parker from three weeks ago would hate me so much right now. He would hate Tim, too.

"You're doing great, Jake," Tim says as I sign and date the paperwork. "Keep it up."

I can't believe that just happened.

We're in the kitchen cleaning up after lunch. I haven't said anything to anyone about what happened earlier because I don't know how to bring it up. I don't want to make anyone upset, especially Jordan.

"How'd your sesh with Tim go today?" Jordan asks as we wash our dishes over the sink.

"Good," I say, hoping the conversation will end there.

"Yeah?" she asks, glancing at me with a raised eyebrow. "What happened?"

Shit. I can't lie to her. I'm freaking out inside because I have no idea how she'll react to this.

"I'm being discharged after next week," I say in one breath.

Jordan immediately drops the glass she's washing on the floor and it shatters, so of course all eyes are on us now. I feel like such an asshole for telling her, but I feel even worse about the fact that I'm leaving her in a week. She just looks at me, holding back tears, and shakes her head. I feel like I'm abandoning her, and I know that's how she feels, too. God, this sucks.

"Jordan, I'm . . ." I try to say, but my words trail off as she bolts out of the room.

Samantha goes after her, and I just stand there by the sink, frozen and at a total loss for words. I don't know if that could've gone much worse than it did.

TWENTY-ONE

It's almost midnight, and I'm pacing around my room at Path with my phone in my hand while I wait for Cat to respond to my text.

Heeey . . . can we FaceTime? I need to talk to you about something.

Cat's response appears.

Yes. But I'm in bed RN. Give me 5.

I send a thumbs up emoji back.

I can't stop thinking about what happened with Jordan at lunch today. I haven't seen her since then. I assume she's in her room, but I don't know for sure. God, I hope she didn't leave. I want to talk to her, but I don't know what to say, and I definitely don't want to make her more upset.

Cat's calling. I sit on my bed and prop my phone up against my laptop screen. I take a deep breath, and I answer.

Cat appears on my phone, and I wish you could see how different she looks now than she does during the day. She doesn't have any makeup on, and she's wearing a pair of reading glasses that instantly age her ten years. She greets me with a yawn instead of a normal 'hello.' She looks so tired.

"It's usually like pulling teeth just to get you to answer a phone call," Cat says. "Now you want to FaceTime late at night? Are you okay?"

"Yeah, yeah," I assure her. "I'm okay."

"Oh, good," she says, relieved. "You already look better. Healthier."

I try so hard not to react to that. I know she means well, but my eating disorder just interprets that as 'you look fatter,' and it's so hard not to believe that.

"Sorry, I said the wrong thing, didn't I?" Cat says, pressing her hand against her forehead.

"No, no, you're fine," I insist, trying not let us get caught up on that tangent.

Of course Cat didn't mean that I'm fat, I have to remind myself. There's too much I want to talk about to make a big deal out of something like that.

"I – um – I'm actually calling to tell you that I'm being discharged after next week," I say, not sounding as excited as I probably should.

"Oh, wow," Cat says. "Jake, that's . . . That's great. I'm happy for you."

"Thanks," I say, and Cat narrows her eyes at me because she can sense that something else is bothering me.

"Is there something else you want to talk about?" she asks.

I nod and sigh. I'm glad that Cat knows me as well as she does because it would be so much harder for me to talk about this shit if she didn't.

"I told my friend today that I'm leaving, and she got really mad," I explain.

"Someone got *mad* because you're doing well?" Cat says, and it's like I can see the smoke coming out of her ears as she starts to get heated. "Jake, that's ridiculous."

"It's not that simple," I say. "She's like, my best friend. We started treatment together, and we've gotten really close . . ."

"So she's upset that you're leaving before she is," Cat says, starting to understand the situation better. "That's tough."

"I don't know if I should try to talk to her or if that would just make things worse," I say with a frustrated sigh.

"I would give her some space," Cat says. "I think you could use some space, too. You need to focus on you right now."

Cat's probably right. I can't just not care about Jordan though, and I kind of hate that about myself. I care about other people more than I should, and I don't care about myself as much as I should. I guess that left the door open for something like an eating disorder to walk into my life.

"Give her some space," Cat says again. "She'll come around."

"I hope so," I say.

"Have you talked to your parents?" Cat asks.

I shake my head no. I haven't. I don't see a point in talking to them right now. They have their own shit to worry about, and it's not like they spend enough time with me to understand what I'm going through anyway.

"That might be for the best," Cat says, and she yawns again. "Like I said, you need to focus on doing what's best for you right now. You have a lot on your plate as it is, and your parents can be a lot to handle."

"Oh, trust me, I know," I say.

"Keep doing what you're doing, Jake," Cat says with a smile. "I'm prouder of you than you'll ever know."

"Thanks," I say, and I smile because hearing that from Cat means more to me than it would coming from just about anyone else.

"Oh, and for future reference," Cat adds, "don't call me past eleven. I'm always here for you, but I wake up at five every morning. I need to sleep, too, you know."

"Got it," I say, laughing. "Sorry."

"Good night, Jake," Cat says.

"Good night," I say, and I hang up the call.

TWENTY-TWO

I'm at lunch the day after the incident with Jordan, and no one's talking. I haven't seen Jordan since she stormed out of the kitchen after lunch yesterday. I don't know if she's even here anymore.

"What's the deal with Jordan?" Lauren finally asks.

"I think she's in her room," Morgan says.

"I hope she's okay," Tori says, concerned. "I know yesterday was rough for her."

"She wasn't at breakfast either," Lauren says through a mouthful of BLT. "I guess she's not eating today."

"She'll have to make up the macros for whatever she misses from meals today," Samantha says.

"She's gonna have to drink so many supplements," Lauren says, and her eyes widen as she comes to that horrible realization.

Lauren looks disgusted just thinking about whatever 'supplements' they make you drink here. Tori does, too. It's like they're both having war flashbacks all of a sudden.

"They gave me one a few weeks ago," Tori says, looking mostly at me, "and I've followed my meal plan to a T ever since. They're *that bad.*"

"Have you had one yet?" Lauren asks me, and I shake my head no.

I've been eating (and drinking) everything Jessica's given me so far because I didn't think I had there was an alternative to my meal plan. I mean, I know we all have eating disorders here, but it's crazy to me how some of the others straight-up refuse to eat sometimes – especially if those 'supplements' are as awful as Tori says they are.

"They're so gross, dude," Lauren says, shaking her head. "Avoid at all costs."

Copy that. That shouldn't be a problem for me. I've made it this far without having to drink a supplement. I wish I could drink some of them for Jordan though. I haven't even had one, but I already know she's going to hate it at least as much as she hates those cheese sticks.

Tim comes into the kitchen, which is weird because usually it's just the dietitians in here with us. He looks stressed out about something. I see him flash an apologetic smile at the dietitians before briskly walking over to me.

"Jake, can you come with me please?" he says, and somehow I just know that shit's about to hit the fan.

I nod and follow Tim out into the hall. I have no idea what's going on, so of course I'm coming up with the worst possible scenarios in my head, and for some reason, like half of them involve someone dying.

Tim doesn't say a word to me as we walk down the hall towards his office, and that makes me even more nervous about what might be happening.

We turn a corner, and I can't believe who I see through the window in Tim's office. It's Cat. She looks pissed. I don't know what the hell she's doing here, but I know it's not good.

We walk into Tim's office, where a fuming Cat with her arms crossed and one of her heels tapping on the floor impatiently.

"Feel free to take a seat," Tim says to both of us but mostly to Cat.

I take a seat in my usual spot, but Cat stays put.

"I'm fine, thank you," she says coldly.

"What's going on?" I ask.

Tim looks at Cat, and I can tell he's trying to decide whether he should tell me or if she should. Cat's too pissed off to even look at him, so Tim takes the lead.

"There's no easy way to tell you this, Jake," Tim says, "but somehow, word got out that you're here . . ."

"And now the whole world knows," Cat says, never one to beat around the bush.

Oh my god. It's like I can feel my heart sink into my chest as soon as she says it. This can't be happening.

Cat holds up a copy of *The New York Post* or one of those garbage tabloids for me to see. I don't think it's possible for the headline on the front page to be any bigger or bolder than it is.

Jake Parker's Secret Battle Against Anorexia
<u>REVEALED</u>!

I shouldn't even be surprised that they used one of the worst pictures of me that have ever been taken. One is from the red carpet at that awards show six months ago, and the other is a photo of me from the week before I started treatment. I hope the asshole paparazzi who took that picture is happy with himself. I look horrible – I can see that now. I have to look away because I can't stand to look at it any longer.

This might just be the worst thing that's ever happened to me, worse than the eating disorder itself. I didn't want people to know about it for the same reason that I don't want people to know that I'm gay. People love labels, and once they've given you a label, it's almost impossible to take it off.

Cat slams the newspaper down on Tim's desk.

"I need to know who's responsible for this so we can press charges," Cat demands.

"Cat . . ." I try to say something to calm her down, but she doesn't let me.

"No, Jake," Cat says furiously. "This is serious. This is exactly the kind of story that could end your career just like that."

She snaps her fingers.

"I've seen it happen, Jake," Cat says. "If we don't do something about this, it *will* happen to you."

I don't know what to say to that. Cat can be dramatic sometimes, but she wouldn't say that if she didn't believe it to be true. If my career crashing and burning is the price to pay for recovery, then it's worth it. I've been doing this to get my life back, not taken away.

"I assure you that we'll take appropriate action if we find that someone here is responsible for this," Tim says calmly.

"I don't think there's any 'if' about it, Tim," Cat fires back. "I should have known something like this would happen. These people aren't your friends, Jake. They only care about themselves."

"You don't know that!" I shout, and my voice cracks the way it does when you're using every ounce of strength you have to hold back from crying.

"Really?" Cat asks. "If they cared about you, would this be on the front page of every tabloid in the country?"

I can't answer that. I don't know why someone would do this to me, especially someone here. I can feel myself getting angrier than I've been in a while. I want to prove Cat wrong, but I can't because she's right. No one who cares about me would do something like this.

"You can't trust people, Jake," she says. "That's the lesson here."

I basically trusted everyone. It's hard not to trust people when you spend as much time with them as I have here. I guess that was my mistake.

"Jake, do you have any idea who might have done this?" Tim asks me, trying to steer the conversation in a more productive direction.

"No," I say. "I have no idea."

I think about it some more, and then all of a sudden it hits me like a brick. I don't know why it took me so long to realize it because it's so obvious to me now.

"Lily," I blurt out as soon as it comes to me.

"Lily?" Tim asks, surprised. "Are you sure?"

Oh, I'm sure. I know Lily act as naïve and innocent as a seven-year-old, but I think I was right on the money when I called her a cryptic bitch.

"She said something super weird on my first day here," I explain, "like she would 'totally keep my secret.'"

I wonder if Lily already knew when she said that that she would end up doing the exact opposite. I hate her.

"Where is she?" Cat asks, ready to resolve this.

Tim gently raises his hand to signal to Cat that she should calm down. He picks up the phone on his desk and dials a number.

"Can you bring Lily to my office please?" he says into the phone. "Thanks."

"You're leaving today," Cat says to me stone-cold.

"But I still have another week," I argue.

"You want to spend another week here?" she asks. "Why, so one of your 'friends' can tell everyone that you're gay, too?"

Fuck. That's something I've never actually talked about with Cat, but I mean, of course she knows. She spends too much time with me not to know. I wish she wouldn't have brought that into this though. I'm having a hard enough time wrapping my head around the fact that everyone knows about my eating disorder. I don't even want to think about what it would be like if everyone knew that I'm gay, too.

"It's bad enough we had to cancel the tour," Cat reminds me. "We can't afford this kind of press right now, Jake. Your career is on the line."

That's a really fucking hard pill to swallow. One that no one else here really has to worry about. They don't have the same kind of pressure on them that I have.

Carolyn knocks on the door and walks Lily into Tim's office. She smiles at us to be polite, but I have a feeling she knows what she just walked into because she doesn't stick around for even a minute.

"Lily, take a seat," Tim says, and Lily sits right next to me.

I'm too pissed off to look at her. I don't deserve this. I don't know why she would do this to me. Sure, I've said some things about her that aren't exactly nice, but I've never said anything like that to her face.

"Did I do something wrong?" Lily asks innocently.

This bitch is either a really good liar or she genuinely doesn't know what's going on here. I'm gonna go out on a limb here and say the bitch is a liar.

"We think you may have," Tim says to her, sliding the tabloid across his desk for her to see. "Do you know anything about this?"

Lily looks at it and has the audacity to act completely surprised by it as if this isn't her doing.

"No!" she insists. "I swear, I would never do something like that."

She turns to look at me, and I can see in her face that she's telling the truth. I just know.

"Jake, I'm so sorry someone did this to you," Lily says, and I believe her.

"Thanks, Lily," Tim says, getting up from his desk. "Let me walk you back."

If Lily didn't do it, then who the hell did? She was our only lead.

"I'll be right back," Tim says, leaving me and Cat alone in his office for a few minutes.

Cat looks even more fed up now that we don't we have a lead. I feel horrible. Cat shouldn't have to put up with this. She shouldn't have to worry about me. I'm not worth it.

"I'm sorry, Cat," I say to her.

"For what?" she asks.

"For everything," I say. "If I didn't have an eating disorder, none of this would be happening. I should be getting ready to go on tour right now. Instead, I'm in Phoenix wondering how the hell I'm supposed to recover when it feels like the whole world is just waiting for me to collapse."

Cat bends down to meet eyes with me. Now that we're face-to-face, she doesn't look so mad anymore. She looks sad more than anything else. She sighs.

"Don't ever apologize for what you can't control," she tells me. "It's not your fault that you're sick. Things may not be going the way you or even I wanted them to, but I think you'll find that life has a way of working out the way it's supposed to."

She offers a sympathetic smile, but I don't smile back. I can't because of what I see through the window behind her, and in that moment, it's like my world turns upside down all over again.

Cat stands and turns around to see what I'm looking at. Jordan is outside Tim's office, walking down the hall with Jessica.

I make eye contact with Jordan from where I'm sitting, and as soon as she looks at me, I know. I know it was her. Everything about her screams guilt. She looks afraid and ashamed – and honestly, she should be.

I furiously bolt out into the hall to confront her. I don't think I've ever felt so much anger towards another human being. Cat follows behind me but wisely keeps her distance.

"IT WAS YOU, WASN'T IT?" I scream at Jordan as I approach her out in the hall.

"What are you talking about?" Jordan asks, but it's obvious to me that she knows exactly what I'm talking about.

"You told everyone where I am," I say through gritted teeth. "Didn't you. Now the whole fucking world knows!"

Jessica looks like she wants to say something to mediate, but I give her a look that tells her to stay the hell out of this. She looks genuinely afraid of me. I've never seen anyone look at me that way. Jordan, meanwhile, is on the verge of tears.

"Jake . . ." Jordan says, "I'm sorry."

"You should be," I say coldly.

"I just thought that if everyone knew, then maybe . . ." she starts to say.

"Maybe what?" I ask. "I would freak out and relapse, so then I would have to stay here with you? Is that what you wanted? Do you know how fucked up that is?"

Jordan starts crying now. I made her cry. Whatever. Why should I care? She clearly doesn't care about me.

"Jake . . ." she starts to say, but I cut her off again.

"Save it," I say. "I thought you were my friend."

I did. I didn't just think of her as my friend, I thought of her as my *best* friend. I cared about her more than I did about myself sometimes. I'll never make that mistake again.

"Cat was right," I say. "I shouldn't have trusted you."

I look in Cat's direction, and she immediately looks away like this is too hard for her to watch. I wish she didn't have to. I wish she didn't have to see me fall apart right before her eyes. I know what it was like for me watching my mom fall apart after the divorce. I can't think of anything more painful than seeing someone you care about lose control to the point that they seem to become a different person.

I can't stand looking at Jordan any longer. I was never her friend. I was just stupid.

I turn away from Jordan and head back towards Tim's office.

"Let's get out of here," I say to Cat.

Tim is walking in our direction, but I don't have anything else to say to him or anyone here. I'm so fucking done with this place.

"Jake, wait . . ." Tim says from down the hall.

"Cat," I say again. "Let's go."

I walk right past Tim towards the door. Cat starts to follow, but Tim pulls her aside for a minute.

"Just hear me out," he says to her. "Jake can take the weekend to cool off and figure things out, but I think it's in his best interest to come back on Monday and complete the program."

"I'll let you know what we decide," I hear Cat say, and she walks out the door with me to leave this stupid place.

TWENTY-THREE

I'm in my bedroom at home, alone with just my guitar and my journal. I finish writing a verse of the song I started writing while I was at Path. I sing a little bit of it as I strum the strings of my guitar.

I remember in my first week at Path, Jordan said she felt numb, and I'd never really felt that before, but I do now. I was so angry before, but now I'm nothing. I feel nothing, which makes writing this song harder than it should be. I can't write a song about overcoming something when life keeps throwing more shit at me. Everyone comes to a point where they can't do it anymore, a point where they can't keep fighting anymore, and I feel like I might already be there.

There's a knock on my door, and Cat peeks her head in.

"Can I come in?" she asks, and I nod.

We barely said anything to each other on the drive back from Phoenix yesterday, and we haven't said much to each other since then either. I'm sure she's been keeping her distance because she's afraid I'll lash out at her like I did to Jordan yesterday.

I never lashed out like that before my eating disorder. It's like my eating disorder created this part of me that's meaner and angrier than I've ever been, and when that part of me comes out, I'm out of control. Tim was right about that part of my eating disorder. I thought it would make me feel in control, but the truth is that I feel more out of control with my eating disorder than I ever did before.

I don't feel like the person I was before my eating disorder, and I don't even feel like the person I was yesterday – the person who lashed out at their best friend without even giving her a chance to speak. I don't know what I feel like right now. I just feel numb.

"You okay?" Cat asks, sitting next to me on the bed.

"Yeah," I say just because I know that's what I'm supposed to say.

"You sure?" she asks.

I nod, and I decide that maybe it's okay not to feel anything right now. I need time to figure out how to feel about everything.

"I'm proud of you," Cat says, hugging me from the side.

I try to force a smile, but it doesn't happen. Cat might say she's proud of me, but *I'm* not proud of me. Let's be honest – I haven't done anything worth being proud of in a long time.

"Your parents want to talk to you," Cat says, glancing at about a thousand text notifications on her phone. "They've literally been calling and texting all day."

"I haven't looked at my phone," I say.

"Maybe you should," Cat says, and she unplugs my phone from the charger by my bed and hands it to me.

I look at the notifications on my lockscreen, and I don't even know it's possible for my parents to have texted me as many times as they have in the past twenty-four hours. It's insane. I get that they want to talk to me, but you'd think they would've realize at some point that I don't want to talk to them right now.

"They care about you, Jake," Cat says.

"I know," I say, swiping away my notifications.

I haven't talked to my parents or anyone besides Cat because I don't know what to say. Everyone's seen the headlines by now. Everyone knows what's going on. What else is there for me to say?

"Is there anything I can get for you?" Cat asks.

"No," I say, putting my phone down.

"Okay," Cat says, hugging me from the side again. "Let me know if there is."

She gets up to leave the room, and as she's heading out, a new notification appears on my lock screen. Oh my god. It's a text from Jordan. Jordan texted me.

Even after what happened yesterday, I can't help but smile when I see Jordan's name. Here I was thinking that she didn't care about me and that I might never see her again, and now she's texting me.

I open the notification as fast as I can to read her text.

i love you*, i miss you, and i'm so sorry for what I did

I can see that she's typing a follow-up. I wait for a second, and then it appears.

*platonically.

I start laughing as soon as I see that, and I notice Cat standing in the doorway giving me a weird look.

"Are you sure I can't get you anything?" Cat asks.

"Actually . . ." I say, "do we have ice cream?"

"No, but I can get some," Cat says, amused. "Do you have a flavor preference?"

"Cookies and cream," I say because we all know that I'm trash for cookies and cream-flavored *anything*.

"You got it," Cat says.

"Thanks, Cat," I say, and she heads out, leaving my door cracked.

I look at the home screen on my phone and glance at the Twitter icon. The little notification number by it is literally in the thousands, and it's going up every second. Holy shit. I'm actually afraid to open it and see what people are tweeting about me. I don't know if I'm ready to see my own downfall all over social media.

As I'm deciding whether or not I want to check Twitter, Aaron calls. I haven't talked to him since I left for

Phoenix. I don't know how much he knows or what he's read on Twitter and wherever else people are talking about me. I take a deep breath and answer the call, putting the phone up to my ear.

"Hello?" I say nervously.

"Jake!" Aaron says with refreshing enthusiasm.

Is it possible that he doesn't know? I wonder. He's on Twitter, and it's not like he lives under a rock, so I don't know how he wouldn't know. I guess there's also an outside chance that he knows something I don't because I can't think of a single reason why he'd sound so excited to talk to me right now.

"Jake," Aaron says, "Have you looked at Twitter?"

"No?" I say, confused.

"You need to look at Twitter," he insists. "Right now. Get on your computer and look at Twitter."

"Okay . . ." I say, grabbing my laptop.

I honest to God don't know why Aaron is making me look at this right now. The past couple of days have been a rollercoaster for me to say the least, and I'm ready to get the hell off now. I don't think seeing what everyone on Twitter has to say about my eating disorder is going to make me feel any better about it.

I log onto Twitter and stare at my feed for a second. I don't want to open the Notifications tab.

"Are you there?" Aaron asks.

"Yeah," I say, watching the little number by the Notifications icon go up every second.

"Open your notifications," Aaron says, and I do.

There are more tweets there than I can comprehend, and more are coming in every second, but oh my god. They're nothing like what I thought they'd be. Most of them are from fan accounts, but I stop scrolling when I see some with blue checkmarks next to their names. Holy shit.

@TyraBanks: ILYSM @JakeParkerMusic! Stay strong handsome <3 <3 <3

Tyra Banks tweeted me. I didn't even think she *followed* me. I mean, obviously she knows who I am, but I'm not worthy of a follow from the host of *America's Next Top Model*, which everyone knows is the greatest reality competition show of all time. (Hi, yes, I'm gay.)

@ddlovato: The world needs more people like @JakeParkerMusic. You're beautiful inside AND out. Rooting for you babe! #prorecovery

Oh my god. Demi Lovato. You know how Jordan said something about a Gay Holy Trinity? Yeah, well there's a Disney Channel Holy Trinity too, and Demi Lovato is my Lord and Savior. It's my dream for Demi, Miley, and Selena to form a girl group someday. They'd put Fifth Harmony to shame, and I'm willing to fight anyone who disagrees with that.

@taylorswift: So proud and inspired by @JakeParkerMusic for taking time to focus on his health and recovery. Love you Jake!! Xoxo

WHAT. Taylor Alison Swift tweeted me, Jake Parker, with her actual, verified Twitter account. Okay, yeah, I'm officially going insane. I don't even know what's happening anymore.

I'm crying even more than I was at my first Taylor Swift concert six years ago, not just because Taylor tweeted me, but because of how many people are tweeting me to tell me they support me. I'm even seeing the word "inspiration" being tossed around, which is crazy because I've never even talked about my eating disorder, and suddenly I'm an inspiration to people just because they know I went to treatment.

I forget for a minute that I'm still on the phone with Aaron because I'm so wrapped up in reading through these tweets that are nothing like what I expected them to be like.

You know, as up-and-down and roller coasterish as my life has been lately, I can't say that it hasn't been consistent. Consistently unpredictable.

TWENTY-FOUR

I'm pacing around the patio on the roof of my building on Sunday morning. I'm finally doing it. I'm calling my mom. I don't know if she'll answer. I guess it depends on how hungover she is today. God, I wish she would get her shit together. Everyone probably wishes the same thing for me now though.

"Hello?" my mom finally picks up, and it's exactly the kind of 'hello' you want to hear when you haven't talked to your mom in three weeks instead of the hungover and sleep-deprived 'hello' that I was expecting.

"Hi, mom," I say into the phone.

"Oh my god," my mom says to someone else. "It's Jake!"

"I'm so happy to hear from you, Jake," she says to me. "Are you okay?"

"Yeah, I'm okay," I say.

"Good," she says, relieved. "I'm so sorry about what happened . . ."

"I think I'm okay with it now actually," I say, and I'm kind of surprised myself about how mature I sound all of a sudden.

"Really?" my mom asks.

"Yeah," I say, looking out at the amazing city around me. "Life has a way of working out the way it's supposed to."

Every time I think my life is over, life proves me wrong. I don't know if that's fate or coincidence, but despite everything that's happened, I don't think I can say that I've had a horrible life. If that were true, I would never have gone to treatment, and I wouldn't have the insane amount of support that I have now. That's so different than what I would've told you three weeks ago, or even a couple days ago, but it's so clear to me now.

"I'm so proud of you, Jake," my mom says. "Always. I hope you know that."

"I do," I say, and I mean it.

Maybe people should be proud of me. Maybe I should be proud of me, too. Okay, so I've hit of a lot of low points, but I'm starting to realize that I can't just define myself by my accomplishments like I did before. Even with my music and everything, I wouldn't be who I am if it weren't for what I've had to overcome.

"You know, I've been meaning to tell you something," my mom says. "I started a twelve-step program a couple weeks ago . . ."

"WHAT!" I say so loudly that everyone in L.A. can probably hear me. "Mom, that's . . . That's amazing."

Tim said that eating disorders usually serve some kind of purpose for people. I think alcohol does the same thing. It filled a void for my mom after she split from my dad, and it totally changed who she was. It was really hard for me to watch as a kid.

"I'm twelve days sober," my mom says, and I can hear her start to cry, so of course I start crying, too. "We're both gonna take care of ourselves now."

"I love you, Jake," she says. "I'm your biggest fan, and you can talk to me about anything. I know you have your own life now, but I'm still your mom and you can always, *always* count on me."

That just makes me cry even more. I'm glad I'm the only one up here because I don't want anyone seeing how fucking emotional I am right now.

I care so much about my mom, and knowing that she's gonna be okay and that I can count on her now is amazing honestly, and it's something that I didn't think would ever happen.

"You can count on me, too," another voice on the phone says.

It's Jule. I miss her so much. I wish I could just move her out here with me, but I feel a lot better about her being in Seattle now that my mom is starting to get her shit together.

"I love you guys," I say.

"WE LOVE YOU, TOO!" Jule says way too loudly.

I realize that I'm finally starting to feel better about everything. I know that might sound crazy, but it's true. I'm starting to accept that there are things that I just can't control. I can't change the fact that everyone knows about my eating disorder now. I can't change the fact that I had an eating disorder in the first place. There's a lot that I *can* do though, and I think knowing that is what's keeping me together. I was so sure that I would completely fall apart, but I don't know if I've ever felt more sure of myself in my whole life.

And I have to say, it feels pretty great.

TWENTY-FIVE

It's Monday morning. I wasn't sure if I'd ever go back to Path after everything that happened. I didn't know if I was ready to see Jordan again or if I even wanted to follow through with my last week of treatment, but now I know now that I do.

There's a different kind of pressure on me now than there ever was before, and I think it's a good kind of pressure. If the whole world's watching me, then that means that people who are going through what I'm going through are watching me, too – so I have to keep going. I have to seize this opportunity to reach out to people and inspire people in a way that I couldn't have six months ago.

I was so obsessed with the idea of being exactly like the person everyone wanted me to be, and I was constantly disappointing myself because I couldn't be that person all the time – but now I know that I don't have to be anyone but myself. I'm so lucky to have the career that I have, but that's not all that I am or all that matters to me.

I'm going back to Path today because I know in my heart that it's worth it. I know that I'm worth it.

You have to want it as badly as anything you've ever wanted, Tim told me in our first session at Path. I didn't want to recover then, but I do now. I want it as badly as anything I've ever wanted.

Everyone else is eating breakfast at the table when Tim walks me into the kitchen. I wave to them with a smile the same stupid way I wave to my fans when I first come out on stage.

"See you, Jake," Tim says, and he gives me a parting pat on the shoulder.

"Later," I say, grinning from ear to ear as the other clients all rush over to give me a hug.

I notice the dietitians look at each other to decide whether or not they're going to try to stop everyone from swarming me, but they decide it's not worth it.

I make eye contact with Jordan, the only person still sitting at the table with the dietitians. I motion for her to come over to get in on this massive, totally platonic group hug. She gets up, and by the time she's near me, the rest of the group has dissolved and is moving back to the table, leaving just me and Jordan standing there.

Everyone's looking at us, including the dietitians, and for some reason, I feel like they expect us to kiss like we would if this were the ending of a Disney Channel movie or something.

"I'm glad you came back," Jordan says to me.

"Me too," I say.

"I'm sorry that I . . ." she starts to say, but I pull her in for a hug to let her know that it's okay.

"It's okay," I tell her. "We're okay."

I can hear Jordan start to cry as her head rests on my shoulder. I don't care that she's crying – I still think she's a badass, and I totally stand by that.

"I had to drink so many supplements," she says.

"Please tell me they were chocolate," I say as we pull out of our hug.

"Nope," Jordan says. "They were out of chocolate, so I had to drink vanilla."

"Oh god," I say. "I bet that was so gross."

"Yeah," Jordan says. "I'm not missing a meal again."

"Good," I say with a smile. "Me neither."

I glance over at Jessica, and she winks at me with a smile. I keep thinking about that look on her face when I confronted Jordan the other day how she looked so terrified of me. I'm glad I came back so that that won't be the way we remember each other.

I might only be here for one more week, but I'm ready to kick this week's ass and to make the most of the rest of my time here. I'm ready to soar, goddammit.

EPILOGUE

"Performing for the first time this year with a brand new song, please welcome the *incredible* Jake Parker."

I'm getting ready to go on stage for the first time in a long time. I can feel the adrenaline rush through me as on stage, Tyra Banks introduces me to a crowd of thousands of people and millions more watching from home.

I thought I would be nervous, but honestly, I've never felt more ready for this. I've never felt more sure that this is what I want to do and that this what I was meant to do with my life.

I'm not the person I thought I wanted to be before my eating disorder, but that's okay because I think the person I am now is better and stronger anyway.

I hear thousands of people cheering for me, and they're not cheering for the Jake Parker I thought everyone wanted me to be. They're cheering for the Jake Parker that I am today, and knowing that gives me all the confidence I need to go out on stage and give it everything I've got.

The first and only time I've shared this fwith anyone was when I sang some of it in front of Jordan when we were at Path. I can't see her from here, but I know she's in audience, and so are Cat and Aaron and Tim and Jessica. I didn't feel like I could perform again without having the people who helped me through everything here with me.

My parents are here, too, and so is Jule. They're gonna stay with me for a few days until they go back home to Seattle, and I can't believe I'm saying this, but I'm actually looking forward to spending time with them.

It's so cool to be singing something that says so much about who I am and what I've been through. I've always loved performing, but it's like my music is more than just music now. I'm not singing about what Taylor Swift or any other musician could sing about. I'm sharing my story and my experiences with people through my music, and that's so much more fulfilling than anything I was doing before.

About halfway through the song, I take a step back from the microphone and move my guitar so that it rests on my back. I tell my band behind me to stop for a minute.

I didn't tell anyone I was doing this, so I hope I don't get kicked off the stage or something, but I have something that I want to say, and I feel like now is the right time to say it.

"As you guys know," I say into the microphone, "I've been through a lot since the last time I was on this stage. Some of it was good, and a lot of it wasn't. But I know now that the good couldn't have happened without the bad.

"So to anyone out there who's struggling with something like I have," I say, "I want you to know that you have the power to change your life."

"And once you find the strength and power within yourself to get better, hold on to it and never let go," I say, my eyes welling up with tears. "Because that's when your life changes for good."

Everyone in the audience claps and cheers for me, and somehow, I just know that what I'm saying is making a difference and that someone out there needed to hear that.

I bring my guitar back over my shoulder and nod to my band to pick up where we left off. Maybe I'll look back at this in ten years and have a different perspective, but right now, I feel like this is the best I've ever performed and probably the best I've ever felt.

I feel . . . incredible.

ACKNOWLEDGMENTS

Acknowledgments... Where do I even begin? There are so many incredible people in my life who deserve to be acknowledged for their support and for their contributions to this book, to my life, and to my recovery from anorexia.

Thank you to my mom for encouraging me throughout my life to be true to who I am and to pursue what makes me happy; to my dad for respecting the person I've become; and to my grandparents and my entire family for their unending support in my life, my career, and my recovery.

Thank you to Andrew, my brother, for being someone that I can always, always count on for advice and support. I've learned so much from you and have gained so much respect for you as we've gotten older, and I honestly couldn't ask for a better brother or a better best friend than you.

Thank you to my friends – Madison Portman, Zoe Fox, Ange Crockett, Lane Levitch, Bayley Killmeier, Ang Toich, Emma Pommering, Brendon Post, Drea Kirby, and so many more – for being some of the most loving and supportive people on this planet. I'm so grateful to know these people and to be able to call them my friends at this time of my life.

Thank you to Kelly Trautner, Calvin Timbrook, Karli Alger, Whitney Hill, Taylor Lechner, and everyone else at The Center for Balanced Living. Words can never do justice to the incredible impact that these people and my experience at The Center have had on my life and the lives of so many others who have struggled with an eating disorder.

And last but by no means the least, I'd like to thank Liz Roberts, Erin Vlach, Stella Kanchewa, Chris Schultz, Dr. David Banas, Dr. Thomas Hubbs, Chris Henrie, Lydia Rall, Austin Moore, Jay Davis, Ryan Jay, Leigh Scott, Marissa Holt, Ashley Patrick, Felicia DeRosa, Amanda Spencer, Michael Schnieders, Jaelani Turner-Williams, Lynn Slawsky, Kristen Portland, Camryn McPherson and everyone else who has been a source of support and encouragement for me in any way, even if just by text or Facebook comment. You are all deserving of the love and support you give to me and to others, and you all mean more to me than you'll ever know.

CPSIA information can be obtained
at www.ICGtesting.com
Printed in the USA
FFHW020523240419
51956179-57364FF